Calling Wren

Neil O'Donnell

Argus Enterprises International
New Jersey***North Carolina

A-Argus Better Book Publishers, LLC

For information:
A-Argus Better Book Publishers, LLC
9001 Ridge Hill Street
Kernersville, North Carolina 27285
www.a-argusbooks.com

ISBN: 978-0-6157468-2-1
ISBN: 0-6157468-2-9

Book Cover designed by Dubya

Printed in the United States of America

Dedication

This book is dedicated to Dr. Albert A. Dekin, Jr.

Beyond being an accomplished archaeologist and educator, Professor Dekin was a mentor who made sure his students gained an understanding beyond the textbooks. Thank you for everything, Professor Dekin.

Wendat
[Huron]

Great Lake of
the East

Thunder Falls

Neutral Nations

Wenro

Seneca

The Veil of
Tadadaho

Lake of the Erie

Erie

Haudenosaunee Confederacy

Andaste

[Susquehannock]

↑
N

Journal of William Sullivan

AD 1655

AD 1655

Chapter 1

Lavender and crimson hues emanated from the edge of the growing cloud cover, last reflections of the setting sun's rays. Above, stars searched out openings amidst the clouds seeking those on Earth awaiting guidance and protection. The Sky, ever-present, reigned as the greatest of the 'Oki,' the spirits that inhabited all things. On this autumn evening, Sky's attention seemed fixated on a village of Erie a day's journey south of Thunder Falls.

The village, resting after great celebration and sacrifice, lay quiet, the songs of crickets and frogs offering the only audible greeting to Sky and Moon, the latter's luminance steadily increasing as twilight gave way to night. Cast on the wings of the wind, sounds of the agitated creek, southwest of the village, soon carried into the song; harmony filled the air, if but for the night.

Rock's Blood, war chief for the village, stood vigil along the creek's edge. Gazing up at Moon, Rock's Blood looked for any sign of promise that his fallen enemy, a young Seneca warrior, would find the path to the afterlife where the village of ancestors awaited.

"Lead him to the further-world, Sky," Rock's Blood said as he stepped barefoot into the creek, its chilled waters invigorating his senses. "He fought and died well." Navigating over a slick, shale creek bed, Rock's Blood fought the steady current finally ending his trek at the creek's center. Saturated by the autumn-cooled water, his deerskin leggings numbed Rock's Blood's legs. Yet, his passion for the rite kept the cold at bay allowing the Erie war chief to maintain focus.

Long moments passed as Rock's Blood sang of the Seneca's courage and audacity throughout the skirmish and subsequent torture imposed by the Erie clan mothers. Then, the rite finished, Rock's Blood grasped the fragment of antler strung around his neck. Well-worn after years of handling, the antler charm remained Rock Blood's sole connection to his companion spirit, Rook.

"Seek the fallen, Rook," Rock's Blood uttered into the wind. "Bring to Sky all who wander." Moments passed as the warrior contemplated the village's torture of the fallen Seneca. "He died well," Rock's Blood whispered, turning over his hand to reveal a leaf from a silver maple, which cradled a lock of the fallen Seneca's hair. The Erie war chief then bent over and gently rested the burdened leaf upon the creek's surface.

"May you freely join the ancestors," Rock's Blood said while watching the maple leaf ride the current.

"Father? Will Rook answer?" a voice asked from the shoreline, the person obscured by shadows and a mix of maple, pine and oak trees. Rock's Blood stared intently again at the antler charm resting against his bare chest, momentarily ignoring the voice. He then looked past the clouds, focusing on the Host Star, which illuminated Sky's northern realms.

"We shall see, Wren. We shall see," Rock's Blood replied to his son's question, his eyes ever fixed skyward. Wren, after quickly removing his own moccasins, entered the creek to stand at his father's side. Together, father and son watched the stars for answers.

"Look," Rock's Blood said, extending his left arm and index finger west towards the distant cloud formations. "Do you see Sun's lingering rays? The crimson shades are fading first. Sky has found the fallen warrior," Rock's Blood whispered. "He will find space in his ancestral house."

"What of Rook? Did he help the Seneca?"

"Who's to say? Though, I doubt Rook would have ignored the journey of such a devout warrior. My guess is that Rook took the Seneca in his arms and carried the fallen to Sky. In any event, our vigil is over. There's nothing more we can do here."

Grasping the charm and pressing it against his left breast, Rock's Blood let the pulse of his heart console Rook as he walked cautiously to the shore; Wren followed close behind. Once he was out of the water, Rock's Blood removed his leggings, dried off his limbs with a deer hide, and then donned a robe made of raccoon skins. Wren, who likewise dried off, contemplated his father's actions while putting on his moccasins.

"Why did you release the Seneca's lock of hair, Father? Won't that permit the Seneca's spirit to return and claim revenge on us?" Without turning to his son, Rock's Blood contemplated his actions before speaking.

"I don't subscribe to such notions, Wren. Sky watches over us all, even the Seneca peoples, and I doubt if Sky welcomes our fighting. I believe that most of us act with good intention and that Sky wishes that all women and men of good purpose be freed to travel to the further-world."

"But the Seneca, he killed members of our village. How can we let the enemy be free to harm our people again?" Rock's Blood turned towards his son. Placing his arm on Wren's shoulder, the war chief took in the young Erie's gaze. Wren's ever-questioning eyes stared back at Rock's Blood. Both father and son stood approximately six feet in height and maintained braided, brown locks of hair that extended down to their mid-backs. Likewise, each possessed warm, brown eyes that reflected a calm and patience that rivaled any of the Erie. In Wren's eyes, Rock's Blood saw a spark of hope that peace and understanding would ultimately come to all Iroquoian-speaking people.

"War is sometimes unavoidable, Calling Wren. I'm sure this Seneca thought attacking us would save his people from harm, just as we fought to preserve our people from the Seneca and their Haudenosaunee allies. Perhaps our compassion will ease the Seneca's pain and need for vengeance. Come. Let's worry about this no more."

Cool autumn air their only companion, Rock's Blood and Calling Wren walked northward through the woodlands. Within little time, the two Erie came to the base of the knoll upon which rested their home and the palisade that encircled the entire village. Constructed of felled trees two to three inches in diameter, the palisade once stood seven to ten feet high. How-

ever, recent attacks by Seneca fighters, armed
with iron and copper trade axes, left large sections of the fencing in need of extensive repair.

"Ever vigilant," Rock's Blood whispered as
he rested his right hand on a damaged section of
the palisade. Without another word, father and
son marched through the entry corridor to the
village. A narrow passageway lined with hewn
saplings, the entry corridor curved around the
southeastern edge of the palisade for fifty feet.
Residents walked the corridor in order to reach a
village with seven longhouses upon a three-acre
area. Enemies had yet to get that far.

Along the interior of the palisade, platforms
lined the walls from which archers could unleash
countless arrows to repel attacks. In the latest
attack, one Seneca, the young warrior the clan
mothers ordered executed, made his way to the
midpoint of the corridor before falling from arrows. Having reached twenty-five feet beyond
any previous attacker, the Seneca crawled another ten feet before capture. The Seneca's failure
showed the effectiveness of the corridor.

"Their axes sliced through so easily," Wren
said as he reached forth and touched nearby cuts
to the palisade.

"Tools from the white-kin," Rock's Blood
said as he considered the flow of European trade
goods that seemed to reach all Iroquoian-

speaking nations save for the Erie. "I'm surprised the Seneca didn't use a single *ouraouenta* [fire-arm]. If they had, I doubt the palisade would have held." Wren considered his father's words as they walked to a courtyard in front of the village's longhouses, where the Seneca's remains now smoldered. Here, stale air laden with scents of *oyngoua* [tobacco] and burned flesh accosted the two wanderers. For a time, Wren stared at the Seneca's remains, his focus on the wounds inflicted to the deceased's extremities; the charred torso made it impossible to see the arrow wounds that marked the Seneca's torso. During Wren's observance, Rock's Blood looked skyward, examining pyre smoke as it danced amidst the clouds overhead. Like a compulsion, the Erie's war chief pulled a pinch of tobacco from a small pouch and threw it onto a mass of burning embers, hoping to assuage any malevolent spirits that might seek to harm the Erie villagers.

"He died well," Rock's Blood uttered once more as if to countermand the anger of the clan mothers who sought to trap the Seneca's soul for their own purposes.

"Calling Wren," a calm, chilled voice called out, jarring father and son from their reflections. "Your mother's been looking for you."

"Grandmother," Wren said as he turned in the direction from which the voice called; his eyes quickly rested on his maternal grandmother, Hawk's Wing, who stood little more than five feet tall. Though nearing her fiftieth winter, Wren's grandmother appeared as agile as ever, and her dark, brown hair, missing any white strands, only heightened the illusion that she was younger than Rock's Blood. Wren swiftly moved towards his grandmother and hugged her warmly. Clad in a raccoon-skin robe, Hawk's Wing looked prepared for a formal gathering, which Rock's Blood did not fail to notice.

"Run ahead," Hawk's Wing said, pulling away from her grandson to stare into his eyes. "Such somber eyes for such a jubilant spirit," she said quietly while Wren simply smiled at her. "Go on now, before your mother sends out the entire clan to search for you." Wren nodded before sprinting northward towards the Deer clan's longhouse, his home since birth.

"Matron, it is good to see you," Rock's Blood said taking a formal tone for the conversation he knew would take a serious turn.

"Rock's Blood, son of the Hawk Clan, we require a moment of your time," Hawk's Wing said dryly. As if on cue, the matrons of the other Erie clans emerged from the darkness. As to their rank as elder mother of their respective clan, the matrons donned raccoon-skin robes and carried a staff of carved maple.

The matrons encircled the war chief they had appointed eleven summers past. Rock's Blood bowed his head, waiting for permission to speak.

"The Seneca nearly breached the palisade this time," the matron of the Raccoon clan said acerbically; Rock's Blood focused on the ground, waiting to speak. "Even their arrow-heads are metal now. The white-kin's technolo-gy will be our downfall. Why have you been unable to acquire these materials?"

"We trust your counsel, Rock's Blood," Hawk's Wing said, abruptly ending the other matron's tirade. "But, we're concerned that our enemies and allies have secured fire-arms and copper axes. We can survive without the metal pots and glass beads, but the white-kin's wea-ponry is..."

"Useless, matron," Rock's Blood whispered as he lifted his head and stared at his wife's mother. "I mean no disrespect, but battle is what I know, and these weapons that you fear have limitations. This stone knife cuts well enough," he said, pulling a dark-gray, chert blade from a deerskin pouch. "It can bite into bone and hide, just as any metal blade can." The war chief took a moment to show the blade to every one of the gathered matrons. "The stone cuts cleaner than the white-kin's blades, and the escarpment near Thunder Falls provides an endless supply of the stone. The copper and bronze implements you so desire, matrons, are limited to the morsels the French and English release to our allies and enemies."

"You have yet to answer the question, Rock's Blood. Why have you failed to bargain with the white-kin?" the matron of the Turtle clan asked. "It's as if you are purposefully avoiding contact."

"Our allies and enemies have prevented the English and the French from entering our lands. Yet, even if the Wendat and Seneca allowed the white-kin to travel here, I would not have bargained." A gasp from the collected matron's made clear Rock's Blood's predicament; his brazen defense of his actions was wearing on the matrons' nerves. "The Wendat are dispersed, scattered across the northern lands, unable to survive without the metal tools and other white-kin resources you so desire. The Haudenosaunee nations, I fear, will soon find it difficult to recall the manufacture of stone implements and ceramic vessels, technologies we take for granted. Copper and bronze are exotic, matrons, but stone and clay are durable and renewable. We can remain Erie as long as we hold to our traditions.

The Haudenosaunee Confederacy, like the Wendat Confederacy, is losing the knowledge our peoples long held dear. What will happen to them when all their elders are gone and the white-kin withhold the metal?"

"To think that by isolating us, our enemies were sheltering us from destruction," another matron mused.

"And the fire-arms?" Hawk's Wing asked trying to keep the discussion focused, her tone as calm and cool as ever.

"I can loose a quiver of arrows in the same time it takes to discharge a fire-arm twice, and the arrows fly truer," Rock's Blood said. "I also don't need the white-kin's help to fix a warped arrow or bow." A mix of scowls and low murmuring amongst the gathered matrons made clear their disdain for Rock's Blood's assessment of the Erie's predicament as well as for his perceived inaction. He moved quickly to resolve the clan matrons to stay the course of isolation.

"The Haudenosaunee and Wendat confederacies were so focused on killing each other for beaver pelts and the white-kin's metal trinkets, they are forgetting the old ways," Rock's Blood said silencing the clamor. Fearing the matrons' wish to trade with the English and French, he employed a new argument. "Copper axes and pots in place of pottery and stone; the Oki remember disloyalty and have answered in kind, matrons. That is why the Wendat fell and the Seneca and their compatriots will eventually be cast aside by the white-kin."

"What of the Dutch?" Hawk's Wing interjected, her patience worn. "What if we seek to ally with them?"

"The Dutch have not the strength of the other white-kin nations, and the French will soon be as weak in their hold of the northern woodlands. The English have the upper hand now, thanks to the Haudenosaunee."

"Perhaps we can send envoys to the Seneca, make a new bid for peace," the Turtle clan's matron said as she moved close to Rock's Blood. Her forehead furrowed, she reflected the angst felt by all the matrons.

"I fear that is no longer a possibility, matron. When we killed the Onondaga's chief, we destroyed any hope of a truce. Anenraes was one of their most revered warriors; the Onondaga will never forget nor forgive his death. They will push the Seneca and other Haudenosaunee nations to attack us until the last."

"Opening our homes to the fugitive Wendat likely made matters worse," the matron of the Fox clan said poignantly. "I'm sure the Haudenosaunee think we are gathering strength to oppose them, much as I warned would happen."

"The Wendat have ever been our allies," Hawk's Wing retorted. "We could not ignore their plight." Taking time to rein in her anger, Hawk's Wing stared down each of the gathered matrons, imposing her will as she often did. "The Wendat have our protection, always. To turn them aside would bring the wrath of the Oki, which we cannot afford to do. Agreed?" The other matrons nodded in consent; Rock's Blood, meanwhile, stared ground-ward, waiting for permission to speak. "Rock's Blood? When do you anticipate the Haudenosaunee will attack?"

"With the trees leafless, a Seneca war party would have no cover now. We'll have the winter to prepare, whether a defense or an envoy."

"Then let us reconvene in the morning after we've had time to collect our thoughts and our wits," Hawk's Wing said. "Perhaps a night's rest will make things clearer." Bowing to her and the other matrons in turn, Rock's Blood turned towards the longhouses and walked on reassured his words would be considered.

Chapter 2

Wren meandered through the village until he stood before his clan's longhouse. With the structure standing just over twenty feet high and covered with sheets of birch bark, the young Erie remained awed at how the longhouse and its arched roof looked so at home amongst the trees and grass. It was as if the longhouse grew from the soil, as did the corn, which contrasted with the cold dwellings built by the French. Wren saw several of the stone dwellings erected by missionaries; stone, mortar and wood just seemed an unnatural accompaniment to Wren. Resting his hand on one of the longhouse's shingles, Wren put aside thoughts of the visitors' constructions to whisper thanks to the Oki for letting the structure endure the recent battles unscathed.

"Ever vigilant," Wren said as he retracted his hand, repeating words his father spoke earlier. Wren then glanced up at the antlers suspended above the doorway. The antlers, long held by the Deer clan's matrons, were recovered from a buck that survived eleven summers.

Wren contemplated the deer's powerful sacrifice. Corn and squash remained a staple for the people, but the deer always appeared plentiful, especially during the most disastrous times when the winter seemed endless and stores of vegetables were nearly or completely exhausted.

"The deer are a gift from the Oki, given to the faithful," Wren's mother once said. There, staring at the antlers above, Wren prayed he was considered faithful, to the Oki and the Erie.

After several moments of further reflection, Wren stretched forth his hand to the black bear fur covering the entry. Then, pushing aside the fur, he stepped into the longhouse's storage area, separated from the living space by saplings and birch bark and identical to the storage end at the opposite side of his family's longhouse. Here his clan stored baskets of corn and squash along with dried venison. These storage areas, a common element to most Iroquoian longhouses, also housed spears used for fishing and quivers with arrows tipped by gray, stone projectile points, which looked like elongated isosceles triangles, each nearly an inch in length.

For a moment, Wren's gaze focused on a nodule of the gray stone, one of many his clan gathered each Spring and Fall. The stone, a chert

extracted from the escarpment two days travel
north, provided material from which the villagers
made arrowheads, scrapers, spear points, knives,
spoke shaves, drills and even beads. Yet, as durable as the stone appeared, damage from constant use remained inevitable. Here, any member
of his clan could grab a nodule, break off a section, and manufacture whatever implement he or
she needed. The countless cornstalks currently
filling the storage area made it difficult to see the
stock of stone recently acquired. The lone nodule he saw seemed out of place, almost lost.
Wren picked it up off the hard-packed floor and
scanned its surface for signs of human workman-
ship. His young eyes quickly located evidence
of someone's labor.

"This stone has answers for every purpose,"
Wren muttered as he rested the stone back to
earth, a comment his grandmother continually
made whenever she needed to generate a new
scraper for cutting and scraping hide. His
thoughts quickly turned from his grandmother
and the stone when he crouched fully to the floor
of the longhouse. Free of grass from lack of sunlight and the constant footfalls of humans, the
ground appeared as stolid as any tree or stone.
Further contemplation of the longhouse floor
ended when the chorus of voices from the living
quarters grew loud and raucous. Laughter soon

carried throughout the voices as did shouts of names, which belonged to Erie who fell during the recent conflict.

With eyes shut and head bent in sorrow, Wren took a moment to remember the fallen as each name was called. Then, when the roll call concluded, Wren stood, walked to the deer hide-covered doorway, and entered the smoke-filled living quarters of the longhouse he called home.

***

Ash-laden air immediately assaulted Wren's senses as he entered past the hide curtain. Then, after choking on the dense air for a moment, Wren scanned about the structure, searching for an unobstructed path towards his parent's section of the longhouse; not an easy task since members of his mother's clan filled nearly every square inch of the structure's floor. With only the timid light emanating from the fire pits lining the center of the longhouse floor, Wren struggled to visibly identify the occupants. Yet, the familiar voices and Wren's experience maneuvering to his mother's space were enough to guide the young Erie onward.

"Wren!" a woman called out from the darkness of the longhouse. Seconds later his mother's youngest sister, Seerna, stepped into the faint light, proving Wren's assessment of the voice had been accurate. "Your mother has been searching for you for some time. Where have you been?"

"With father," Wren replied. He now stood firm, his head bowed in recognition of Seerna's rank as a clan mother. Knowing Seerna's distaste for Wren's father, he awaited a scolding, but none came. Seerna picked up a small ceramic pot and a wooden ladle from next to the nearest fire. Then, she stirred the contents of a larger pot resting in the fire's coals and spooned two ladle's worth of the corn and venison stew into the smaller pot.

"Hurry and eat this as soon as you reach your mother's space," she said in a motherly-tone. "Get there before your mother does, and you may yet soften her anger when she sees you." Wren nodded and smiled at Seerna before moving on to the middle of the longhouse where his parents and he slept. Once there, Wren sat on the ground just beneath the bench [*Endicha*] where he and his parents quartered. The bench, extending nearly five feet from the wall, was simply one area of a platform that ran along the entire length of the structure and mirrored the bench that ran along the longhouse's opposite wall.

After finding a comfortable place on the ground, Wren spooned out a mouthful of the stew. With winter still weeks away, stores of corn and dried venison remained plentiful as evidenced by the generous amounts of each in the stew. For a moment, Wren thought of the scarcity of food the Erie faced last winter and the Erie lives lost as a result. Seconds later, as a moment of melancholy coursed through him, Wren returned his attention to the stew as well as his surroundings. He might have been sitting in any of the village's longhouses given the symmetrical design of their homes. Aside from the standard use of end storage areas and benches, which ran along the sidewalls of every Erie longhouse, the structures contained other routine elements. For heat and illumination, the clans lit multiple fire pits, set along the central area of each longhouse. Positioned on either side of every fire resided one nuclear family; both families shared responsibility for maintenance of the fire. Individual families stored personal items and slept in these areas. Overhead, in the network of saplings supporting the roof, additional space was reserved for the clan's weapons, tools and hides, which did not fit in the end storage areas.

Wren, once finished with his pot of stew, drank from a pot of water under his family's bench. His thirst quenched, he removed his out-

er-garments before returning to his space on the
longhouse floor. There, bare-chested, Calling
Wren grasped the amulet that hung from the
deer-hide strap wrapped around his neck. The
amulet, a serrated-edged tooth from a shark, was
a gift to him from his beloved, Wind's Whisper.
She never told Wren the name of the spirit contained in the amulet. That revelation she planned
to provide on the night of their union. All Wren
knew was that the tooth was obtained by the Turtle Clan through the trade network that reached
beyond the Great Lake of the East, further than
even the territory of the Mohawk.

"Will you not tell me your name?" Wren
asked as he grasped the amulet with his hands.
Tightening his grip, Wren felt the tooth's serra-
tions piercing his flesh and the traces of his
blood now trickling through his fingers. The
amulet did not respond to Wren; it never did.

"The Oki are not so eager to divulge their
names, my son," Wren's mother said, which
drew his attention immediately. "They only
speak when we are ready to accept responsibility
to protect the portal the amulets open." Standing
almost to Wren's height, Sulvas was an imposing
figure whose resolute disposition and stature im-
pressed even the sternest of clan matrons and
elite hunters. To Wren though, she was his
mother first, a role she never failed to fulfill.

Sitting by her son, Sulvas focused on Wren's amulet while looking for words to assuage Wren's sorrow. Now, as the clan considered Wren of age to wed, she could not avoid the cold reality she must impart upon her only son.

"Wind's Whisper was abducted nearly two winters ago. Even if she were alive, she would have been adopted by one of the Seneca's clans and likely with husband and child. You must move on, Wren. Move on for your sake and for that of the Erie." Sulvas' azure eyes cast against her long, chestnut hair, conveyed a true compassion to Wren; he knew she grieved with him.

"I was promised to Wind's Whisper, Mother. I was promised through your oath and by my heart to Wind's Whisper, to the Turtle clan and to Sky. Would you have me betray them all?"

"Your responsibility to the people overshadows promises made to individuals or clans, which you know full well. As for Whisper's clan, I spoke with her mother earlier today. We agreed you should wed Whisper's sister. That way, our clan's promise is fulfilled." Sulvas' words stung Wren deeply as his personal promise to Wind's Whisper was what he truly feared breaking.

"I will never love another," Wren said after silently considering his new marriage arrangement.

"That is your decision, Calling Wren," his mother said as she stood and faced him. "Nevertheless, you will obey the clan's wishes." Wren, with bitter resolve, stood before his mother.

"By your command, matron," he said dispassionately before bowing and leaving the longhouse.

***

Wren wandered back to the creek, the one place he found true solace. Sitting on the cobble-laden shore, Wren stretched out his legs until his heels rested below the chilled water. His eyes shut, Wren took every sound that played to the woods. Frogs, crickets and the water itself sang out, their songs lacking a unified theme. Yet, as Wren's own heartbeat settled and added to the chorus, the disparate sounds grew more harmonious. It was in these moments that Wren could easily recall Wind's Whisper; her smile, her laugh, her eyes.

Here, Wren was alive, at peace with both the Oki and his memories of Wind's Whisper. Yet *Time*, the unseen and ever-present enemy, remained relentless. It interrupted the peace bringing forth sorrow and grief. Memory of his mother's words, two years passed, again hammered at his soul. *"The Seneca have taken Wind's Whisper."*

Chapter 3

Wren, exhausted from the day's events and chilled by the frosty air, eventually retreated to his mother's longhouse to sleep. Still angered by Sulvas's tirade, Wren decided to spend the night in the storage area. Wrapping himself in one of the raccoon-skin cloaks stored in the area, Wren sat near the doorway to the inner sanctum, from which emanated heat cast by the interior fires. He was not alone for long.

His canine companion, Jasper, was by Wren's side moments after he entered the long-house. Jasper, the offspring of a wolf and one of the canines brought by the white-kin, stood inches taller than any wolf Wren ever encountered. Covered in a shaggy mismatch of curly gray and black fur, Jasper appeared disheveled and aloof. Yet Wren and the rest of villagers learned Jasper was more than a match for any other canine as he could outrun the others while also bearing a bulk of muscle and sinew, which pummeled anything or anyone Jasper ran into. As the first major frost of Autumn crept into the village, Wren looked to Jasper's bulk for warmth as much as for company.

There, amidst the distant crackling of the fires and beats of Jasper's heart, Wren fell into a deep sleep.

***

Cold, wet and abrupt... the deluge woke Wren as did the muffled laughter accompanying it, laughter that sounded all too familiar.

"Come on, Wren," his elder cousin, Redwing, said. "We've got a longhouse to repair." Huddled tightly in the cloak on the ground, trying to fight off the chilled water's affects, Wren stared up to meet Redwing's amber eyes and mischievous smirk. Then, after contemplating a terse response, Wren's eyes rested on the clay pot cradled in Redwing's arms. With no doubt the vessel once carried the water now covering his body, Wren quickly considered ways to enact some measure of revenge on his cousin.

"Worry about getting even later, Wren," Redwing said as he rested the pot on the ground. "You know, if you want, I could always build you a bench to sleep on out here. I'm sure the matrons wouldn't mind," Redwing chided as he helped Wren to his feet.

"Are you trying to get rid of me, cousin?" Wren asked knowing Redwing and he were like brothers and would never be separated.

"Come on, the sooner we get to the Fox clan's longhouse, the sooner we can get some corn chowder in you to warm your bones." Wren nodded as he hung his wet robe on a near-by support post before grabbing a dry one. Then, after exiting the storage area, the cousins walked west towards the Fox clan's dwelling.

The Fox clan's longhouse received the most damage during the latest raid. With the addition of two recent births to that clan, the village planned to repair and expand the longhouse sim-ultaneously. As always, the Erie villagers would work collectively, repairing the structure as if it sheltered their own clan.

As Wren and Redwing made their way to-wards the village's west end, a number of males, young and old, joined them. All the clans would be represented in the effort, with every male first meeting in front of the Fox clan's longhouse for morning nourishment. For the morning meal, Wren, Redwing and the other laborers consumed a helping of corn chowder filled with venison. Wren, after inhaling some of the hot broth, closed his eyes and quietly rejoiced as the hot liquid reached out to his frigid bones and muscle.

"Feeling better?" Redwing asked as he held out a piece of cornbread for his younger cousin. Wren waved off the offering choosing instead to drink again from his pot of broth, corn and venison. Once warmed, Wren used a wooden spoon to fish out chunks of venison and kernels of corn. The meal satisfied his hunger quickly and warded off the morning chill, but their rest was short-lived. The assembled villagers, men and women, young and old, quickly dismantled the end storage area of the Fox clan's longhouse. Afterwards, the strongest men from the village took time to sharpen the ends of stout saplings, which would serve as secondary support posts for the new addition.

Wren, Redwing and several other youths, meanwhile, dug out holes in the ground where the posts would be set. The collective action of the villagers emphasized the symmetry of Erie life. While clans usually adorned their respective longhouses in unique ways, often with ancestral totems or charms, the architectural design of longhouse superstructures was quite standardized. Each longhouse stood twenty-five feet wide with benches running the length of each wall, extending outward five feet. Likewise, every nuclear family was reserved a ten-foot long bench area for eating meals, sleeping and the storing of personal items. Only the lengths of longhouses varied, which reflected the number of clan members. If a clan's numbers grew too large, the village constructed a second longhouse for the clan. The Fox clan's longhouse was nearing the point when a second longhouse would be needed. Even as the elder males of the village secured wall supports for the new section, Wren internally questioned whether such an effort should already be taken as the new addition was less than ten feet from the palisade.

"Redwing! Wren!" exclaimed Redwing's father, breaking Wren's concentration on the longhouse's dimensions. "Get to the rafters and tie off the supports," he said as he helped three other villagers finish the positioning of saplings for extending the existing roof supports over the new section.

"Looks like we're sky-walking today," Wren commented enthusiastically as he and Redwing moved towards the main supports of the new construction. After removing his moccasins and slinging a deerskin pouch filled with basswood cordage over his shoulders, Wren effortlessly climbed one of the stoutest supports until he reached the upper rafters nearly fifteen feet in height. Redwing, meanwhile, climbed up cautiously, stopping to rest at the halfway point.

"Need help?" Wren asked, feeling avenged after his morning dousing at Redwing's hands.

Ignoring the taunt, Redwing finished his climb before starting to tie newly added wall supports to the rafters.   Wren smiled, taking note that Redwing started with the lowest of the supports. Their work and Wren's amusement were short lived.

"ROCK'S BLOOD!" exclaimed a voice from the southeast, its source obscured by a dense grove of spruce trees. Everyone stood still while the voice cried out twice more before the audible struggle of feet through foliage guided every set of eyes to the source of the voice. Gasping for air, Vulcar emerged from the woodlands and dropped instantly to the ground. Amidst endless gasps, the shirtless, scared and windless youth cried the war chief's name again before the Erie present surrounded Vulcar and attempted to calm him.

"Seneca... approach... from the east... near the upper creek," Vulcar said in hushed tones as Rock's Blood knelt by his side. With a quick nod to two of the gathered elder males, Rock's Blood initiated a flurry of activity.

Twenty-one of the village men, Rock's Blood included, grabbed bows, quivers of arrows and clubs stockpiled near the entrance of the village before running east towards the oncoming Seneca force. With only a club in hand, Rock's Blood scanned the crowd of youth before following his compatriots. His eyes ultimately focused on Redwing.

"Secure the village and set archers to the interior scaffolds. Defend the matrons," Rock's Blood commanded before sprinting into the eastern woods. Redwing wasted no time.

"Carry Vulcar inside and rouse the village!" Redwing exclaimed, his eyes staring down two of the older boys. Without hesitation, they hoisted Vulcar, wrapping the injured Erie's arms about their shoulders and dragging him into the entry corridor. "Secure the weapons!" Redwing then cried out. Those assembled, mostly boys and young men, grabbed the remaining clubs and bows set at the village's entrance before bolting to the safety of the palisade. Wren, after grabbing two quivers and a bow, watched the ordered dance of the Erie defenders. Amidst the call of birds and the scent of charcoal-laden air, fear mounted and hampered the movements and facial expressions of everyone. *"Was this the end?"* he wondered before a young boy's voice heralded the loss of all hope.

"Redwing! Your grandfather escorted a group of matrons to the field earlier, and they haven't returned," the boy said just as a scream carried on the wind, emanating from the south where their cornfields rested.

"Sky defend us," Redwing muttered as desperation took hold of his mind. "Tell the others to close the gate and defend the walls!" Redwing yelled, his fiery gaze cast at the boy who fled without hesitation to carry on the order. Without another word, Wren and Redwing, with bows and quivers, ran south while the village prepared for a battle that never came.

Chapter 4

Gromar's greatest joy was in storytelling. Every morning, with an escort of villagers both young and old, he headed to the fields recalling Erie history, mythology and philosophy for every open ear. Dependent on a staff for walking, Gromar's hesitant gait, along with his leathery skin and shoulder-length, snow-white hair, projected an air of wisdom, which all the villagers and clan matrons respected.

"What shall we speak of today?" Gromar asked at the start of every morning's trek, encouraging one of the assembled youths to ask a question about the Erie's history. "Ask and I shall answer you." Ever benevolent, Gromar would stop his trek, lean on his maple staff and eye any questioner who dared speak, begrudging no query for Gromar was a knowledge-keeper, a role he intended to pass on to his grandson, Redwing. It was his responsibility to relay tradition and history, which included the origins of the Erie Confederacy, the rise of the Oki, and the founding of the Earth.

Few questions came this morning as it was to be the last trip to the fields for the harvest season. Today, Gromar and his entourage's concerns focused more on acquiring any remaining gourds, beans and ears of corn.

"What we find today may carry us through the winter," Gromar remarked, addressing the concerns of a young girl who questioned the scouring of the fields now disheveled by earlier harvesters. Turning over felled cornstalks, Gromar and the other assembled villagers recovered the few remaining crops missed by previous field excursions. First emptying four large cornhusk baskets of their ash contents, children filled the baskets with roots, gourds and corn while several women spread the ash over the fields. The ash, an amalgamation of charred tree limbs and leaves, would help replenish the soil's nutrients for next year's crops, but Gromar reasoned the next season would be the last this field would be productive. Wandering on his own, Gromar searched through weeds and cornstalks while reminiscing about times as a child when he helped his mother and the village women collected corn, tubers, sunflower seeds, squash and other crops the Erie depended on. After his eleventh summer, Gromar left harvesting behind to hunt with his father. Yet, he never forgot that the labor of the village's women provided the bulk of their foodstuffs.

"Recover every seed, every squash and every tuber," Gromar said as he pulled a small, rotted squash from amongst the foliage, recalling the words his mother said at the start of every harvest. Pulling the seeds from the vegetable's now putrid insides, Gromar shook off most of the gelatinous residue that held to them before dropping the seeds into the deer-hide pouch slung over his shoulder. The seeds secured, Gromar looked at the remaining mass of squash in his hand. "Old and tired," Gromar whispered as he considered his unseemly connection to the gourd. He then went about collecting the remnants of the Jerusalem Artichoke crop. Once an invasive species amongst the Three Sisters, these hardy tubers were now welcomed cultigens, which Gromar relished. Pulling out the nearest Jerusalem Artichoke by its base, Gromar examined the plant's white, asymmetrical root. The Jerusalem Artichoke, usually standing over five feet high, bore yellow flowers in the summer, which Gromar often picked for his mother. For a moment, he thought of earlier days, when the field was ripe with pumpkins, beans and a golden sea of corn. His quiet contemplation ended abruptly.

Thwack!

An arrow slammed into Gromar's chest, the force of which forced Redwing's grandfather to the ground. Gromar's collapse, a flurry of arrows and a chorus of cries from the charging Seneca alerted the Erie villagers of the coming storm. Yet, after the arrows hit their marks, few villagers remained to react. The Seneca invaders wasted no time in reaching the Erie, clubs raised to kill the elders and subdue the younger women. To the dismay of the invaders, the attack quickly unraveled as Erie arrows soon rained on the Seneca from behind. Redwing and Calling Wren arrived on the winds of hope.

***

Wren followed Redwing's flight without a word, the duo cutting through the familiar woodlands in near silence. Only the hollow echo of each drawing an arrow from their bark-lined quivers resonated through the air. Then, just as they reached the clearing at the cornfield's northern edge, Wren and Redwing readied their bows for combat. No amount of readiness would have prepared them for the scene unfolding in the fields. Three Seneca invaders, clad in hide parkas and moccasins, were standing over Gromar's lifeless body and smashing into the knowledge-keeper's remains with their clubs.

Redwing and Wren loosed their arrows without any further assessment of the turmoil. Redwing's arrow bit into the shoulder of one of the Seneca, which knocked the Seneca off balance and to the ground mid-swing. Wren's target was not as lucky.

"Fly," Wren whispered as his arrow released. Seconds later, the arrow pierced through a Seneca's back and sliced through the man's heart; the Seneca dropped to the ground as the last standing Seneca called out to his kinsmen. Wren and Redwing now stood against nine.

Discarding his bow, Redwing darted towards the last of the three Seneca who desecrated Gromar's remains. Then, dodging the Seneca's flailing club, Redwing rammed into the Seneca's body forcing both men into the dirt. After rolling about for several long moments, Redwing disarmed his enemy before landing a blow that dazed the Seneca. Aware the remaining Seneca would be on him quickly, Redwing cursed and spit at the prone enemy at his feet before striking a deathblow to the Seneca's head. Now, club in hand, Redwing readied for the coming wave of invaders, but Wren had already cut into their number.

As Redwing wrestled with the nearest Seneca, Wren looked to the others now alerted to their presence. For an instant, time seemed to stop allowing Wren to capture the moment in memory. All about lay Erie villagers, their garments soaked with blood. In the distance, the three remaining villagers, young females, were escorted towards the eastern woodlands bound for adoption or sacrifice.

"May the Oki save us," Wren said as he threaded his next arrow, determined to kill as many of their enemy as he could. His second arrow struck true, felling one of the approaching Seneca. Redwing was then up and engaged with two Seneca while four others charged Wren. Their number was down to three after Wren cast one additional arrow to the wind. He then gripped his bow as if it were a club, bracing for the coming Seneca assault. He would get in one swing before the Seneca overwhelmed and subdued the young Erie, pummeling him into unconsciousness.

Chapter 5

Wren drifted between Dream and Wake, his desire for rest and an overwhelming pain preventing either state to prevail. The Darkness did not help matters. He knew his eyes were open, but no light was visible, not a star or hearth, neither Sun nor Moon. Prone on a grassless patch of earth, fear wracked at Wren.

"Where is this?" Wren asked aloud, his voice soon echoing as if confined in a cavern. As if in reply, a form, bathed in a pale blue luminescence, materialized before him. With great effort, Wren raised his hands to block the light until his eyes adjusted. Recognition came quickly; before him stood the tortured Seneca his father freed.

"You must wake now," the Seneca said, the spirit's voice barely more than a whisper. The apparition then extended his hand to Wren, which the young Erie took without hesitation. "You are not ready for this yet," the Seneca said while pulling Wren off the cold ground. "You must wake."

***

"I must wake," Wren uttered as consciousness returned. In waking, he also felt an on-
slaught of pain in his limbs, torso and head.
Dusk or dawn, he could not tell, but enough light
was present for Wren to see the bruises and cuts
covering his body. He tried to lift himself upright, but Wren found movement difficult;
spruce-root cordage bound his hands and feet.
Awareness and memory returned.

Wren relaxed to the cold, hard ground,
which was covered in grass, ferns and dandeli-
ons. Looking skyward, Wren watched dark gray
clouds infiltrate the white cloud cover and seemingly chase away the light. He now knew it was
dusk, and a storm from the lake was coming,
fast.

Wren's focus then diverted to voices nearby,
voices speaking an Iroquoian dialect he followed
only with difficulty. His vision blocked by a
cluster of ferns, Wren could not determine who
spoke or how far away the man stood, but he
knew the spoken words were uttered in anger,
anger directed at Wren.

"Are, are you all right, Wren?" Wren, startled, twisted his head towards the familiar voice.
Redwing, similarly bound, lay heaped on the

ground close by. Wren's cousin also appeared scarred from the battle.

"I'm okay," Wren said between deep breaths. Just beyond Redwing stood two Seneca armed with bows. Their hawkish gaze made it clear that escape was impossible.

"Where are the others?" Wren asked as he looked back to his cousin.

"They've been taken on ahead. They're to be given over to the Seneca matrons, for adoption." Redwing laid back and stared up at the clouds at which time Wren caught a glint of tears ebbing from Redwing's eyes.

"I'm sorry about your grandfather, Redwing." For long moments, neither said another word, each intently listening to the conversations between their captors. "What are they saying? I can only make out part of it. Seneca?"

"They're not Seneca, at least not the ones speaking. They're Onondaga, and they are discussing how best to torture us," Redwing replied, his gaze never turning away from Sky. "They seek vengeance for those we killed in the field." Redwing's words weighed heavily on Wren; death never felt so eminent.

"What do we, we do?" Wren asked, his breaths heavy.

"There's nothing we can do," Redwing answered, his eyes finally turning to meet Wren's.

***

The Seneca and Onondaga men soon turned their collective attentions towards their Erie captives. First using chert knives to cut the spruce-root cordage securing their legs, the Seneca jabbed at Wren and Redwing with spears until the captives were standing. Then, with Seneca and Onondagas standing at their sides, Wren and Redwing were prodded along a well-worn path. Exhausted, Wren found it hard to keep pace, but whenever he slowed, the Seneca to his right would pull on Wren's arm, urging the Erie onward. A number of times Wren or Redwing slipped and fell to the ground, the darkness obscuring ditches and rocks. The Erie were quickly pulled to their feet in those instances and led onward by the Seneca who were quite familiar with the area. Soon, the Onondaga members of the party, even unhindered, struggled to manage the path, which required the lighting of a few torches. The light illuminated the surrounding woodlands, which were eerily silent. From Wren's vantage point, they were surrounded by a mixed woodland of maple, birch and pine trees, the heights of which rose and fell by the incline of the drumlins the trees covered.

Marching on, the Iroquoians, friend and foe alike, kept to the marked trail silently, save for the occasional jesting by the Seneca regarding the Onondagas' clumsiness. Wren started to feel as if he was with an Erie hunting party, returning from a successful deer hunt. Nostalgia soon fled as the path ended at a clearing before a great palisade, which towered over a large bonfire.

***

The ravenous fire scorched timbers as quickly as the Seneca set each upon the growing fire pit. Wren and Redwing looked on as the Onondaga separated from the Seneca while the Seneca labored at the fire. Wren tried to listen to the conversations of his enemies, but the crackling and roar of the fire made his already weak grasp of the Onondaga dialect an impossible communications barrier to breach. Redwing faired better.

"One is owed to us!" one of the Seneca matrons barked at the Onondaga. The Onondaga reverently bowed towards the matron; they would not question a matron's command no matter her nation affiliation.

"Prepare them!" One of the Onondaga then ordered. At nearly six feet in height, the Onondaga towered over his kin and all the Seneca.

Donning a beaver fur cloak over a deerskin tunic and breeches, the Onondaga looked regal, like a chieftain of chieftains. As Redwing and Wren were roughly grabbed by the other Onondagas, Redwing swore that this Onondaga would bear the brunt of Erie vengeance over the death of his grandfather, Gromar.

First dragged in front of the fire, the village on the far side, Wren and Redwing were stripped of their garments amidst a flurry of blows to their abdomens and extremities. Then, their limbs numb from pain and exhaustion, the two Erie collapsed. Wren took the time to regain his breath, the final few fists knocking out his stores of oxygen. Redwing, meanwhile listened intently to the Onondaga as they negotiated with the Seneca.

"Anenraes must be avenged, matron," the beaver-robed Onondaga said as he approached the Matron. Covered in a bearskin cloak and with a necklace of bear claws, Redwing had no doubts about which clan the matron represented.

"Your vengeance is most assuredly warranted, but you shall not have both. One shall join the Bear Clan; do what you will with the other."

"What are they saying?" Wren asked, his breathing now relaxed, more rhythmic.

"Quiet," Redwing said as he continued to eavesdrop on the negotiations conducted in the Onondaga dialect.

"Matron, we will do as you command, but both should be punished for the attacks," the Onondaga said, his head ever bowed towards the Bear Clan matron. For long moments, the matron considered the Onondaga's comments. Her answer did not surprise Redwing.

"Agreed," she said before turning towards the gathered Seneca. "Prepare them!" The host of men grabbed Wren and Redwing and dragged them before two lines of women, men and children. Each held branches from trees, including hawthorn branches, and every Seneca and Onondaga screamed in defiance, cursing the Erie nation through words and song.

"What now?" Wren asked, though he was familiar with the rite.

"Now, we run the gauntlet," Redwing answered as he stumbled to his feet. Standing still for but a moment, Redwing looked into the faces of those about him while Wren struggled to his feet. In the distance, just within the realm of firelight, Redwing spotted the Bear Clan matron about who stood seven other women, each donning a necklace symbolizing her respective clan. These were the matrons of the eight Seneca clans: Wolf, Turtle, Beaver, Bear, Snipe, Heron,

Hawk and Deer. Here resided the power of the
Seneca. As with the Erie, the matrons dictated
the way of the people. Without a word, Redwing
bowed to the matrons; their detached stares never
flinching.

"Wren, are you ready?" Redwing asked his
younger cousin.

"I am with you, brother," Wren answered,
knowing the next steps the two took led to suffering and death. Redwing smiled and nodded at
Wren, pride welling within.

"Strength through silence, little brother,"
Redwing replied before turning and running between the two lines of Seneca and Onondaga.
Aside from several muffled grunts, Redwing remained silent as wood sliced, bruised and
pierced his flesh. Dropping twice, Redwing rose
quickly and continued on until he reached the far
side of the gauntlet. The crowd, still cursing
through word and song, then turned their eyes
and bloodlust towards Wren.

"Strength through silence," Wren whispered
as he too bowed to the matrons before charging
between the two lines of enemies. The strikes
came without mercy and ripped at every inch of
his flesh. Thorns, knots and branches battered
Wren's body, drawing blood from his wounds
though not a cry from his lips. Twice he
dropped to the ground after a club strike to his

gut, but he stood again and continued under a deluge of spit and curses. On the far side, Wren collapsed by Redwing's side. His breathing strained and erratic, Wren fought to calm himself. The first torment completed, he wondered what was yet to come.

"Well done, little brother," Redwing said as the two Erie locked eyes once more. As Wren regained his breath, Redwing listened to the commotion and conversations amongst the enemy throng. The chief of the Onondaga was negotiating again for one of them. Talk turned towards the felling of Onondaga at Wren's bow; Redwing's cousin was to be executed.

Filled with adrenalin, the Seneca and Onondaga embraced one another in jubilation. All was in chaos. Nearby, several armed youth stood, unaware of Redwing's attention. The plan was set.

"Wren, listen," Redwing said as he turned to face his cousin. "We are well east of Thunder Falls. If you travel southwest, you'll reach our village."

"What?" Wren asked between gasps for air. Redwing looked at his cousin once more before offering a response.

"Live free, live Erie," Redwing said. Then, smiling briefly, Redwing vaulted up and into a nearby Seneca boy. Grabbing the startled youth's hawthorn branch, Redwing then turned towards the Onondaga chief.

"Gromar!" Redwing yelled as he whipped the branch across the Onondaga's face. The branch's thorns bit deep into cheek and nose. Startled, the Onondaga chief collapsed, but only for seconds. As Redwing continued to swat at his target, the Onondaga grabbed a chert blade from his belt before charging up at his Erie attacker. Bruised and exhausted, Redwing did not have the strength to defend against a skilled fighter. The Onondaga quickly penetrated Redwing's haphazard swings before plunging the stone blade into the Erie's chest. Together, Redwing and the Onondaga fell to the ground. While still conscious, Redwing could do nothing but feel the chert blade twisting in his chest. Redwing looked up into the Onondaga's scarred face and smiled as his last breath left him.

"No!" Wren exclaimed as he tried to rise to Redwing's defense. He immediately was subdued by nearby men who punched and kicked Wren until he collapsed. From the distance, Wren heard the shouting of a female who called out for silence. His eyes cast skyward, he could not tell who spoke until a Bear Clan matron stood over him. After looking over Wren's torn body, she reached down and grasped the shark tooth around Wren's neck. With a quick yank, the necklace broke; his companion spirit was now in enemy hands.

"He doesn't need his eyes to serve as a father!" the Onondaga Redwing had injured exclaimed as he walked into Wren's line of sight. For a moment, Wren felt disconnected from the soil and woodlands. He felt dead as the sounds of the villagers, their sneers and laughter, went suddenly silent. Then, a piercing cry heralded the coming of Sky, who now came in the form of a red-winged blackbird.

The bird circled above Wren, its mesh of black and red hues clear against the moonlight that pierced the dark clouds. Mesmerized, Wren simply watched the bird soar until the haunting bellow of a human returned him to Earth.

"Enough!" cried out the Bear Clan matron. "Do not spoil what the Three Sisters have sown, unless you want to replace the Erie's eyes with your own." Her last words caused a chilly silence among the gathered men, while the other matrons maneuvered to stand behind the Bear Clan matron. The Onondaga turned and stared at Wren, his anger evident behind his strained, brown eyes. Then, after kicking Wren in the side, the man turned toward the matrons.

"My apologies, matrons," he said, his head now bowed and his arms limp at his sides. "My anger bested me, and it shall not happen again.

"Bind him with the other slave," the Bear Clan matron said.

Without another word, the Onondaga chief knelt by Wren's side and punched him full in the face, knocking the Erie captive unconscious.

Chapter 6

"You are not alone, Calling Wren," the delicate voice whispered. Entombed in darkness, Wren felt at ease, comforted, as the voice guided him to consciousness. "Look for me by starlight," the voice uttered as it faded into echo.

"Stay, please stay," Wren called out, tears welling in his eyes.

"You will never be alone," the voice said. Then, for a moment, the darkness parted for a flash of light within which Wren saw a gigantic fish break the surface of a great body of water. At over ten feet in length, the fish was larger than any Wren had ever seen let alone caught. For a moment, the creature appeared to float in the air providing Wren a good look at its entire body. Its eyes were darker than midnight, and its dorsal surface was a dark, blue-gray, much like the chert the Erie used to make arrowheads. The beast's underbelly, however, was as white as newly fallen snow. Captivated, Wren considered the beast's duality: monstrous and yet agile, beautiful yet horrifying. Cleary a creature built for the attack, yet Wren felt no malice from the beast.

"I am here, Calling Wren," the great fish said before it plunged below the water's surface sending a mist into the air, a mist laden in salt. Then, as another flash of light burst forth, Wren saw the image of a hawk in flight, its talons in full view while the rest of the raptor was a blur.

"Talon," Wren whispered as he reached out to the hawk.

"Wake," a new voice said, pulling Wren's attention from the hawk and the great fish. "Wake."

"Father?" Wren asked, as the new voice was barely audible. Wrapped in pain, Wren strained to open his eyes. Comforted by the familiar cracking and scents of a fire pit, the young Erie braved the final steps to full consciousness. The air that greeted Wren was warm, but oily smoke from the fire made breathing difficult, the least of his discomforts. Dressed in only a loincloth, Wren was chilled by the hard-packed sod floor he rested on. Yet, before he could address his need for clothing, Wren suddenly had a new concern. Before him, amidst the flickering shadows of the small, circular, bark-covered lodge, stood a cloaked figure. Rock's Blood always said it was easy to tell someone's intentions and heart by his eyes, yet this figure's eyes were hidden beneath the folds of a black hood. Wren went to stand against the figure, but he found his hands bound to one of the structure's roof supports. Frantic, Wren pulled at the cordage holding him captive, but the spruce-root bindings held. The figure moved closer, which only increased Wren's straining. It was then he heard the figure speak in a deep voice that seemed calm, contrite. Wren understood some words the figure, a man, spoke; the words were definitely Iroquoian. Yet, the mix of Iroquoian dialects made it difficult for Wren to understand until the man focused on the one non-Erie dialect Wren clearly understood.

"Are you all right?" the man said in clear Wendat speech. Wren nodded in reply, uncertain if spoken words were advisable. The figure moved closer until the firelight clarified the man's stature. Near six feet in height, the man's attire made clear his affiliation. Before Wren stood a Black Robe; a Jesuit priest.

The priest knelt before Wren and placed a small ceramic cup to the Erie's lips. Wren drank deeply, the cup's water quenching his thirst.

"French, Black Robe," Wren said after swallowing the cool water.

"Black Robe, yes," the man said as he sat before Wren. His accent was unlike any Wren had ever heard; neither French, nor English, nor Dutch.

"What are you?" Wren asked, fearing he was in the hands of a newfound enemy. The man simply smiled.

"I'm a wanderer from far over the water, lad. I'm Father William Sullivan from County Cork, Ireland, and I am at your service."

***

Wren took a few more draws of water from the offered cup, all the while questioning what his next move should be. Then, as exhaustion and pain reclaimed Wren's body, the young Erie laid his head back to the hard-packed earth upon which he rested. William stood up and moved over to the far side of the structure, reaching down to the ground for a bundle. The priest returned with one of the wool blankets woven by the European invaders, an item Wren's father warned him to avoid at all costs. Frantic, Wren tugged hard on his bindings while backing as far from the priest as possible.

"What's wrong?" William asked, stopping feet from the Erie prisoner.

"English blanket?" Wren asked, his eyes never diverting from the dark dyed blanket.

"Ah, I see your concern," William said as he squatted down to the ground, drawing no nearer to Wren.

"You see? Then why do you hold that blanket close? Do you not fear death?" Wren's rapid questions were answered by a quick smirk from the priest as well as a quiet chuckle.

"I heard such stories when I was a boy," William said as his demeanor soured into a grimace and chilling tone. "Beware English gifts, my mother would say. Many the times I heard my elders warn that the English would hand out diseased blankets to spread death amongst their enemies, charitable acts to hide monstrosity."

"Then why accept such a gift?" Wren asked, his eyes still fixed on the blanket in William's grasp.

"The English are a calculating and relentless enemy, capable of cruelty and malice, a truth they've directed towards my people more than any." The priest's eyes then welled with tears, and amidst a span of silence, Wren saw grief and despair in William's deep, brown eyes. Then, after clutching the wooden cross round his neck, William seemed renewed with hope.

"There are limits to even English barbarism, my friend," William said as his voice and ease returned. "I have no doubt some English commanders considered such a devious ploy, but not even the English would be so cruel to act on such plans." William then held out the blanket towards Wren and waited for the Erie to respond.

As if a doorway had suddenly been opened, Wren felt the chill in the air and earth; he nodded at the priest hoping William's faith in English morality was not misplaced.

"I'd cut you free of your bonds, but the Seneca threatened to kill the other Erie captives if I did so," William said as he covered Wren with the blanket. The priest then walked over to a bear fur and wool blanket on the far side of the structure, removing his hood to reveal shoulder-length, dark-brown hair. Within seconds, William was resting under the blanket, his eyes cast towards the roof and the solitary hole that permitted ventilation of the fire pit's smoke. Wren averted his own eyes to the gap in the roof, searching for answers and solace. It was evening, certainly, but no stars permeated the black veil of night; all was clouded by smoke. Then, a single snowflake penetrated the roof and smoke and floated down to within inches of where Wren lay. He watched as the limited heat of the lodge dismantled the snowflake's crystalline composition, leaving but a smear of water upon the dirt floor.

"It's been snowing heavily since you were brought in," William said without turning towards his fellow captive. "You are here to stay."

Chapter 7

Wren's dreams were shattered, the priest's words driving any last vestiges of hope into nothingness. As sleep came in short cycles, so too did a flurry of nightmares that generated images of torched Erie villages, Wren's family and friends bound for servitude or sacrifice. Even more frightening were the visions of plague-scarred villagers too sickly to care for one another. *A premonition of the end?*

The haunting of Wren's thoughts ended abruptly as a Seneca kicked him to consciousness. Wren's eyes opened to the image of an elderly man squatting down towards the captive Erie's hands. With a quick cut with a chert blade, the Seneca freed Wren before exiting, speaking briefly with the priest as he did so.

"If you run, the captured women will die," William said, words that pulled Wren's focus towards the Jesuit. There was to be no escape, a realization that now brought surprising calm. Still prone amidst the wool blanket, the still crackling fire the only sound puncturing the air, Wren looked again towards the gap in the roof.

Night still reined, though stars now penetrated Sky's shadow.

"Live free, live Erie," Wren whispered as the loss of Redwing returned. The air itself carried the scent of charred flesh, an odor all Iroquoians knew well. Wren knew that somewhere, Redwing's remains smoldered atop a dying fire.

"Please free him, Sky," Wren whispered, tears flowing from each eye. "Let him not be ensnared by the Seneca matrons."

"Who was he?" William asked, a question that scared Wren. Was it a trap, this question from a Jesuit sorcerer?

"He was my cousin," Wren answered, unwilling to offer up Redwing's name.

"You need not speak his name," William said, his view too returning to the stars visible through the roof. "The Huron warned us to not press for names of those we met."

"The Huron?" Wren asked, wary that the priest was referring to some spirit who was betraying the Erie.

"The Huron, those like you who dwell north of the neutral nations," William said as he cast a look of confusion towards Wren. "The ones that speak as you do and live in the villages of countless longhouses. Do you truly not know them?"

"For one who knows so many tongues, you are quite careless in your studies," Wren said amidst a flurry of chuckles. These 'Huron' you speak of call themselves the Wendat. They are like sisters and brothers to us." Wren suddenly felt shame for his jesting and turned to offer an apology to the priest. Yet, words failed Wren as he watched the priest stab at a rectangular item with a feather. "What are you doing?" Wren asked.

"Correcting my journal," William answered without diverting attention from his writing. After recording 'Wendat' into the next open space in his journal, William flipped to the first page of the leather-bound book to inscribe the Huron's true name on a map William previously made of the region. "Thank you for correcting me." Ever the eager student, William capped his ink vial and blew at the journal's pages to hasten the ink's drying. Once dry, he closed the book and looked towards Wren, whose eyes reflected bewilderment.

"Your people use chert to carve symbols into pottery and stone, yes?" William asked. Wren nodded in reply. "This is the same idea; we draw symbols with dark liquids onto paper."

"Paper?" Wren asked, a question William thought about for long moments before answering.

58 Neil O'Donnell

"Paper is like, well… think of it like thin sheets of tree," the priest said after considering the best way to depict the journal's pages.

"Like the interior side of bark?" Wren asked; William nodded, happy to have found a way to depict his act of writing.

"Something like that," William finally said as he placed the journal into a pocket on the inside of his robe, the one place no Iroquoian or Englishman would check on a Jesuit's body.

"What do you draw?" Wren asked, uncertain of how such a device could further injure the Erie.

"I draw maps of places I go to, record details of my journeys through your lands; I write down the names of those I meet." The last William said with reluctance, knowing the value many societies placed on the power of knowing one's true name.

"Why have you not asked me mine?" Wren inquired after sitting up to face the priest.

"I figured you'd tell me when you were ready." William's words and reasoning put Wren at ease. The Jesuit was much like the elders described; cautious and mysterious, but filled with good intentions.

"My name, friend William, is Calling…"

"Wren," a new voice spoke, its tone melodic, yet set like stone. Wren and William turned towards the lodge's hide covered entrance, now parted by the arm of a figure hidden behind a robe of assorted furs. With the entrance ajar, the growing wind, laced with snow, flooded into the structure, a shrill whistling noting the wind's charge. Rising to their feet, the young Erie and Jesuit stood shoulder to shoulder, prepared to meet the newcomer as allies. Hands covered in mittens, the newcomer's arms moved to secure the entrance's hide covering to keep out the lingering storm. Silence soon reigned, drowning out even the crackling of the fire pit. Then, within the flickering firelight, Wren caught a glimpse of the newcomer's face, adorned with a smile that lit Wren's heart. An instant later, the newcomer stepped closer and removed the robe's hood, revealing a face long remembered and greatly missed.

"Wind's Whisper," Wren said as he stepped forth and hugged the young woman. The tearful embrace lasted long moments, neither wishing to let go. Then, after pulling back to stare into each other's eyes, Wren and Wind's Whisper kissed deeply, both feeling whole once more.

***

"Call me as you once did, my beloved. Tell me this is real," Wind's Whisper said after they embraced once more.

"I'm here, Whisper," Wren said as he pulled his eyes back to meet hers. "And this is as real as Sky." Gently brushing Whisper's hair back, Wren warmed at the sight of the woman he pledged himself to years before. "I love thee" [onnonhé]. Their tender moment passed as Whisper stepped out of Wren's embrace, lifting an open left palm to her love. Her hand was empty save for a clump of deep brown hair. Looking from the hair strands to Whisper's eyes, Wren felt the pain she bore. "Redwing's?" he asked, never doubting the answer.

"I removed the hairs before the matrons ordered the burning of his remains," she replied as her gaze lowered to Redwing's hairs. "I went to release them in the river, but I could not remember the Condolence Song." Her voice broke apart with her final words; Whisper's shame in forgetting the Erie's sacred chant felt like a final betrayal to her birthright. Wren clasped her hands in his and smiled as their eyes met once more.

"Let me remember for you," Calling Wren said before chanting the rite. Father William moved back into the shadows of the lodge, not wanting to disturb the couple. The priest felt Wren's and Whisper's heartache, but he also felt their bond as Whisper's memory and voice soon joined with Wren's. The Jesuit could never recall the words they sung, but he would always remember the love between Wren and Wind's Whisper.

After Whisper's memory of the Condolence Song returned, she embraced Wren again, wanting nothing more than to hold him forever. Yet, fears for his safety weighed on her.

"I must go before anyone notices my absence or finds me here," she whispered to Wren. "I will go to the river now and release Redwing."

"No," Wren said as he pulled away from her. "Wait till the storm passes," he pleaded as their eyes locked once more. Her eyes, brown with flecks of green, enthralled Wren; he did not want to let go.

"Now is the best time; I won't be missed. Besides, the storm is waning... I will be fine. Redwing deserves peace." She followed her final words with kisses to both Wren's hands. "I will be back soon." Whisper stepped away as she wrapped up into her robe; Wren reached out and grabbed her arm before she could leave.

"Matron of the Turtle Clan, I stand ready to serve you," Wren said as their eyes met once more.

"I never doubted that, Calling Wren," Wind's Whisper said before exiting the lodge and disappearing into the night.

Chapter 8

"You okay, Calling Wren?" William asked, his concern growing with every passing moment since Wren last said anything.

"What?" Wren asked, clearly still in a daze. "Yes, why, what?" The conversation was going nowhere quick. William chuckled.

"You've been staring out the doorway for some time now. I just wanted to make certain you weren't going to run off into the storm." William walked up beside Wren and patted him soundly on the back after which he walked over to the dying fire to add a couple logs. "Get some sleep, my friend." Wren stood as the priest returned to the far side of the lodge and went back to sleep. Wren walked over to his own bedding and covered up with his blanket. In little time, he went from certain death to certain love, a move that brought a surge of jubilation to Wren's spirit. The fact that the priest now knew his name was a bit disconcerting, but Wren sensed no malice from the Jesuit. It was as if the priest appeared in time to take Redwing's place.

There, surrounded by his enemy, Calling Wren could not help but feel secure, his love and a new ally at his side. Now, he just needed to find a way to get them all to freedom.

***

The nightmares continued the moment Wren feel asleep. Clad in a bearskin cloak, Wren meandered about his mother's village in search of life. Gripping his cloak tight to hold off the bitter air, Wren continued on until he reached the village's heart where five Erie corpses lay side by side, all bearing scars along their exposed skin. Faces, arms, chest... all were marked by oddly shaped wounds. The air itself reeked of death, a scent that finally forced Wren to move on. Aghast, Wren covered his nose and mouth as he shuffled through the snow-covered ground, but the effort did little to hold back the scent or his cries. Wren's nightmare only worsened from there as he entered his clan's longhouse. All about lay elders, matrons, fathers and children covered with festering soars, their hopeless eyes staring skywards. Wren soon found himself walking amidst the infirmed; not a single villager remained to care for the sick. Moans and shallow breaths called out against the hollowing winds that found the gaps in the longhouse's birch bark shell. It was the first time Wren remembered being in a longhouse without the crackling of a fire offering comfort. This dwelling was bereft of any comfort, any hope.

"Have I found death?" Wren wondered as he walked amongst the sick, searching through the fallen for his parents. His search ended in terror as he reached the last section of bench. Her face covered in welts and blisters, Matron Sulvas lay alone with no fire or furs to warm her. Wren ran to her, cradling her shivering body to his.

"I am here, Mother," Wren whispered as tears flowed from his eyes. Matron Sulvas remained silent, her eyes never turning from the rafters. Wren wondered at his mother's condition. Cold to the touch, her shivering seemed understandable. Yet, as he held her, Wren could see and feel the sweat that drenched her brow. "I am here, Mother," he said again, and again she remained silent.

"Help me!" Wren exclaimed as he looked about the longhouse again. Several times he shouted out, but only the wind answered. Wren looked again to his mother as hope slipped further from their reach. "Please, Mother. Please stay with me," Wren pleaded as Sulvas' eyes closed. He could hear her heartbeat slow with each passing moment; she was slipping away. "Mother!" he exclaimed one last time before she vanished from his arms. Then, after a sudden, bright light blinded him for a brief time, Wren found himself outside the longhouse once more.

Ankle deep in wet snow, his cloak now in tatters, Calling Wren walked about in search of survivors. All he found were fur wrapped skeletons scattered about the village. Tears continued to flow from Wren's eyes as each of the remains included gorgets, necklaces and other adornments, which identified the dead. Numb from the cold and endless death, Wren ultimately made it to the front gate. There, Wren dropped to his knees.

"Why... who?" he asked, his eyes cast upwards to Sky. As if in reply, the palisade vanished to reveal scores of Haudenosaunee archers, their bows drawn with flaming arrows. "No!" Wren exclaimed as he stood, his arms raised in protest; his pleas were ignored. The arrows flew, a hollow wail sounding their flight.

Wren watched the great arc of the arrows soar through the air, the mass of projectiles looking like a burning eagle, the wind piecing arrows moving from a wail to a near screeching reminiscent of a war cry. Turning back towards the longhouses, Wren watched in horror as the mass of arrows struck assembled structures immediately igniting the bark siding. Seconds later, the Seneca and their allies charged into the village

and cast torches at the Erie longhouses in an effort to expedite the burning. Wren could only
watch as his legs seemed frozen in place. Every
man who ran towards Wren ignored the young
Erie until the last man approached, an Onondaga
with hair that appeared as a tangle of snakes.

"Tadadaho," Wren whispered as the Onondaga chief drew closer. Tadadaho said nothing
as he walked by, his gray eyes staring back into
Wren's. Then, after smirking at Wren, the Onondaga chief turned and walked on towards the
now cheering attackers.

Wren watched the Haudenosaunee Confederacy's forces embrace one another in jubilation
while the deafening crackles from the rising
flames drowned out the enemy's shouts. The
Haudenosaunee had won, but the victory was
short-lived.

A loud series of clicking sounds resonated
from the woodlands to the east, drawing Wren
and the Haudenosaunee invaders' attention.
Thousands of red-coated white-kin emerged
from the trees bearing firearms. Maneuvering in
unified steps, the white-kin marched on towards
the village until a solitary voice exclaimed,
"Halt!" As one, the white-kin stopped.

"Make ready!" the voice ordered; the mass
of white-kin raised their weapons in striking
unison. "Aim!" The white-kin's heads tilted at

the new command, again moving as if they were all one in body and spirit. Such symmetry belied the death that awaited.

"Fire!" the voice cried after which a flurry of percussion blasts and storm of musket balls reined all veiled by the darkest smoke. Wren raised his arms in defense, but his effort was wasted. The musket balls passed through him as if he was an apparition. Yet, the Seneca, Onondaga and other Haudenosaunee invaders were susceptible, evidenced by the cries emanating from behind Wren. Turning back to the village, Wren's now opened eyes saw the ground blanketed with torn, broken bodies and streams of blood.

A rhythmic pounding of footfalls pulled Calling Wren's attention to the now advancing white-kin army. *Would any Iroquoians survive?* His question was immediately answered.

A massive wall of water rose behind the white-kin, which the red coats seemed oblivious to. Salt laden air, emanating from the water, soon coursed through Wren's lungs, a sensation both refreshing and stifling. Then, heralded by the cry of gulls, hope returned as the great fish vaulted forth from the water.

"I am still here, Calling Wren," the fish called out before plunging back into the depths.

Once again, the vision faded only to be replaced by the image of a raptor's talons.

"I hear you, Talon," Wren murmured as the wall of water shot forward like an arrow and consumed the enemy forces. The wave then dissipated before reaching Wren. A vision of unfamiliar mountains then replaced the village and earlier carnage. Now Wren saw a group of Erie, his mother included, walking up the a path to the mountain top.

"Survive, Calling Wren," Talon's voice said as all was dark once more.

"Survive," Wren murmured as a more restful sleep took hold, the young Erie's words drowned out by the rich, baritone snores of an Irishman whose nose had been broken too many times to count.

***

Wren's nighttime visions collapsed under an intense force, which seared through Wren's stomach and robbed him of breath. Gasping, Wren clutched at his stomach to quell the pain as consciousness returned. Then, after sufficient air circulated through his lungs again, Wren opened his eyes to see the booted foot that kicked him moments before. Slowly, Wren looked upward until his eyes locked with the Seneca that kicked him.

"Wake, Erie," the Seneca said before spitting at Wren. The Seneca's face bore deep scars under his left eye, as if clawed by panther or bear. The man's scarred face contrasted with the graceful flowing locks of brown hair that stretched down his back. For Wren, the superficial duality of the Seneca was overlooked as Wren's attention focused on the amulet tied around the man's neck. The Seneca had donned Talon, Wren's tooth amulet, the tooth attached to hide strap laden with clumps of hair and severed fingers.

Wren locked eyes with the Seneca for a moment. Beyond the man's Seneca heritage, beyond the fact that Wren felled a number of Seneca during the attack, Wren saw deep hatred in the Seneca's stare. It was not hatred for the Erie or for Redwing, but hatred aimed directly at Calling Wren.

"Get them moving!" a voice from outside exclaimed, breaking the moment. The Seneca replied by simply pointing towards the door. At that moment, Father William walked by, grabbing Wren by the arm as the priest passed between the Erie and the Seneca.

"I'd say he's one for you to stay away from," Father William whispered as he pulled Wren out the door and into the blinding sunlight.

***

The sunlight, intensified by the layers of lake-enhanced snow that now entombed the village, glared at Wren's eyes even as the bitter cold air seared at his lungs. It took long moments before his eyes adjusted and his lungs acclimated. His vision then set, Wren saw the Seneca village in full. Rubbing his bare arms to generate heat, Wren turned around repeatedly as he eyed people, longhouses and animals.

"Come," the scarred Seneca said, pulling Wren from his observances. The Seneca then threw a fur robe at Wren, which the young Erie quickly donned. The robe itself was pieced with an odd assortment of black and charcoal fur, all of which were quite tattered. The Seneca around Wren smirked as he adjusted to the garment.

"So skunks can walk upright," an older male Seneca quipped as he walked by, drawing laughter from the others. Wren ignored them, returning to his scan of the village proper.

The Seneca's home resembled Wren's village in many respects. The village, surrounded by a stout palisade, included a number of longhouses from which arose plumes of dense smoke. Yet, for the general similarities, glaring differences stood out. The longhouses noticeably varied in their widths and heights whereas Erie and Wendat longhouses were built almost ritualistically uniform. Wren soon realized the source of the Seneca's variability. One long-house's roof had partially collapsed under the weight of the new snow. Seven Seneca worked at repairing the damage while other Seneca villagers went about gathering firewood or conversing with neighbors.

"Clans divided," Wren murmured as realization came.

"What?" Father Sullivan asked. "Are you all right, Wren?" Just then, the Seneca prodded the two captives onward towards a nearby longhouse.

"Erie villagers band together to build and repair longhouses; no home is raised without the whole village at hand. Here, it seems clans are responsible for their own needs." Wren finished his reply with a nod towards the damaged longhouse as the Seneca led them passed. Then, after passing two more longhouses, the Seneca led Wren and William through the bear hide covered doorway to the longest house in the village. Wren glanced at the bark shingles above the entrance where the jaws of a bear hung. Into the den of the bear matrons, he and William were about to enter.

***

A conclave of Seneca males led Wren and William through the end storage area of the Bear Clan's longhouse and into the cavernous interior where smoke and dank air reigned. William coughed deeply upon entering the living space while Wren seemed unaffected. Oily smoke clogged the air in all longhouses, Erie and Haudenosaunee alike, a castoff from the fire pits lining the central corridor. Iroquoians adjusted to the environment centuries before, while the European interlopers seemed unable to cope with the conditions. Wren held back a chuckle as he turned and patted the Jesuit on the back until William's coughing ceased. It was then that Wren turned and choked himself as he stared into the eyes of the Bear Clan's members. Their eyes were tired, hopeless. What's more, the inhabitants of this longhouse displayed a variety of tattoos and piercings that, while Iroquoian, spoke of a mix of nations. Just in the immediate spaces around him, Wren could see women, men and children of Wenro and Wendat heritage, survivors of the endless wars with the Haudenosaunee.

"So what have you brought me?" The question came from an elderly woman seated on the bench, which ran along the longhouse's north wall. She was shrouded in a thick, black fur, while around her neck rested a thong adorned with thin, copper tubes interspaced between bear teeth. All remained silent as the attention of those gathered gazed upon the woman who clearly was revered by all. She stood, a stout maple staff tightly clasped in her right hand for support, after which her dark, gray eyes observed the Erie and the Jesuit. All heads, save for the Jesuit's, bowed towards this woman, though no one answered her.

"Has the Windigo stolen your voices? Who are these persons?" clearly angered, the woman scanned the assembled, her stare more than any could bear for long. She approached Wren and William slowly, the silence remaining. Wren kept his eyes lowered, awaiting judgment from the matron while William looked back at her as one of the Seneca moved forward.

"These are the captives the Onondaga have given over, my matron," said the mid-aged male who dared approach. He was clad in deerskin, as were all present. Likewise, he bore a cap of bear fur and a necklace with a solitary bear tooth attached. "A Black Robe and Erie to serve you and our clan." The matron's eyes remained fixated on the Jesuit's as she considered the Onondaga's *gift*.

"You are unlike any other white-kin we've encountered, Black Robe," she said as she walked to within feet of William. "Your voice is abrupt, yet kind."

"You are kind to say so, matron," William replied, nodding briefly as he did so.

"We are told to be wary of kindness from the white-kin," she said as she turned and maneuvered back to her bench. "Look about you, Black Robe. Few here trust you or your words. Why should I?" The matron seated herself awaiting William's response. Meanwhile, the assembled feared the coming battle of the white-kin sorcerer and the village's most senior matron.

"You must do as seems best for your people, matron," William replied, nodding again as he spoke.

"Indeed I must, Black Robe," the bear matron said after which she chuckled to every Seneca's dismay. "I know not where you come from, Black Robe, nor do I know your name or purpose. Yet, I do know one thing. Unlike the English and the French, you look upon our women with reverence, not disdain.

"My mother would have it no other way, matron," William replied as hope of survival seemed on the mend. "The women of my people have often stood shoulder to shoulder with the men, in life and war, which is why they are so honored." The Jesuit's tone grew somber, and for long moments, William appeared lost, trapped in some memory. The senior matron of the bear clan and Wren both felt the turmoil within William. Yet, where Wren felt helpless, the matron seemed poised to assuage the priest's pain.

"Cowards and fools are the French and English for their treatment of their women. Your people... my people... we know better." The matron stood and approached the captives once again, leaning heavily on her staff with every step. She stopped before the two, prepared to render judgment. "The English and a contingent of Onondaga will be here within days. Since the English are so keen on driving out the French, I'm sure they will be pleased at your capture, Black Robe. I will hand you over to them. As for you, young Erie, you will stand in place of Featherling, my sister's son. The Erie took his spirit, but through you, Featherling shall return." Wren nodded, familiar with the rite he was now set to take part in. "Return them to the storage lodge until the ceremony." Her judgment cast, Wren and William were led out into the bright light and chill of the winter day.

Chapter 9

Wren and William trudged through the snow in silence, each contemplating his fate. For Wren, his life would be spared, but at the cost of his will and heritage. Father William's fate was less clear, at least for Wren. Would the English adopt William?

"Certainly he would be an asset to the English, for William is a Spirit-Guide," Wren thought. William knew better.

Finally reaching the lodge where he spent the previous night, Wren watched as Seneca men poked stout maple saplings at the wet snow layered upon the lodge's roof. Three men in total, donning black bear fur parkas, danced about as they broke the snow's grip. Occasionally, one would move too slowly and get smacked in the head with snow and slush, much to his companions' delight. Their frivolity reminded Wren of the times he and Redwing cleared off their clan's longhouse, a thought that made Wren forget his cousin's death, at least for a moment.

"Go get your wood, Black Robe!" one of the Seneca exclaimed, pulling Wren's thoughts back to the cheerless present. In response, William headed to a large stack of wood buried by the snow. Digging through frigid slush, William uncovered a couple logs, which he lifted and carried into the lodge. Wren moved to help William, but their Seneca guard stopped him.

"The Black Robe will see to your needs," the Seneca said before leading Wren inside. Once within the lodge, Wren stirred up the remaining embers from their fire pit. Then, after adding three logs to the embers, Wren ignited a fire, which quickly warmed the living space. Meanwhile, William stockpiled fifteen rough-hewn logs to fuel the dwelling's fire through the day and night. Three Seneca remained behind, taunting William as the priest struggled with each armload of wood carried. It was the last armload, William's hands numb and bloodied, that sapped the priest's strength. He dropped the wood and fell to his knees.

"Stupid, Black Robe!" one of the Seneca's cursed as the others laughed. Obviously irritated, the Seneca removed several arrowheads from the deerskin pouch he carried and handed the projectile points to the other two. Then, after quickly turning about, the angered Seneca stepped up to William and kicked him in the stomach. The priest dropped to the floor, clutching his gut and moaning between shallow breaths. Wren answered.

In seconds, Wren was there, throwing his full weight behind a shoulder rush that sent the Seneca into the others. The Seneca recovered quickly, surrounding the young Erie before pummeling Wren to the cold ground. After assuring Wren's submission, the angered Seneca spit at Wren.

"Be careful, Erie," the Seneca said. "You are not one of us yet!" Without another word, the Seneca vacated the lodge leaving Wren and William alone to tend their collective wounds amidst the stiff, chilled air.

***

"You really have a way with people, Wren," William said as Wren wrapped a small deerskin pelt around the priest's hands. The two men laughed, an ease setting about the dwelling. Later in the day, their Seneca tormentors returned with two rabbits and two small pots filled with corn soup. The Seneca Wren assaulted stood by the lodge's doorway the entire time, his eyes ever focused on the Erie soon to be adopted. After the Seneca left, Wren cleaned the rabbits and spitted them over the fire. William, meanwhile, bowed his head as if deep in thought. Wren knew the priest was suffering from a deep pain that made William's physical wounds a minor inconvenience.

"How do you console a broken spirit?" Wren thought as he considered actions to take. Soon after, wise words once spoken by his mother came to mind.

"Food warms the spirit," Wren said as he brought over one of the pots and a wooden spoon to the priest. "You should eat, William." The priest opened his eyes, nodded and smiled as he accepted the offered cuisine. Then, after whispering a thanksgiving prayer, William sampled the corn-laden soup. Wren joined the priest by the fire, consuming his pot of soup in little time. The two passed the evening in silence, eating the rabbits and drinking handfuls of water taken from a provided water-filled pot. Neither seemed ready to fully speak of their pasts, though both were willing to listen.

Time wore down the fire and darkness consumed the sky. Huddling under their own furs on opposite sides of the fire, both men looked skyward, mesmerized by the stars that peered through gaps in the lodge's roof.

"I wonder if we'll ever truly know what the stars are?" Wren asked aloud, breaking the intolerable silence, which only the crackling fire

dared challenge to that moment. His voice preceded a deluge of words.

"When I was a boy, I thought the stars were
the torches of spirits trying to find their way to
earth," William added.

"What did your father tell you?" Wren
asked, his eyes still locked on the stars above.
William laughed before he spoke.

"My father told me I should concentrate
more on tending the fields and fishing. God,
what a terrible farmer I would've made, not that
I was much of a fisherman either." Again, Wren
felt a sorrowful tone in William's voice. *What
darkness still pained the priest?* Wren sought
again to lighten the moment with what seemed to
please the priest most; knowledge.

"My father says the stars and trees and rocks
are our elders who have passed on to the great
village. He says they stand guard, ready to warn
us of danger."

"What danger?" William asked before pushing off the ground and staring through the flames
at Wren.

"They warn of the coming of the Windigo, a
beast that craves flesh and blood." The howl of a
coyote suddenly carried on the air. Father William flipped open his journal to record Wren's
tale while Wren considered the canine's cry and
the evil it preceded.

***

It was a sound akin to the rustling of dried leaves dragged by Autumn winds over the forest floor. It was a quiet rustling, which spoke of the mischief of mice amongst the village's stores of corn, beans and berries. Whatever the sound's source, it drew Wren away from his dreams of family and friends. Opening his eyes, Wren now found himself in a nightmare.

Above him stood countless figures donning wooden masks, each of which captured a human expression, whether it was sorrow, laughter, fear or anger. Wren tried to rise to confront the figures, but he was kept prone by a number of turtle shell rattles, which vibrated in a spastic rhythm that expressed nothing but chaos. The figures then took turns waving their rattles in his face while chanting verses Wren could not understand. After long moments passed, a new figure emerged from the group wearing a dark mask that resembled a bear. The newcomer carried a pipe with a granite, bear-effigy bowl and a long wooden stem. The bear-figure then drew air from the pipe, walked up to where Wren lay, and exhaled the tobacco-laced smoke into Wren's face.

"Come home, Featherling!" the deep voice commanded before blowing more smoke into Wren's face. When the smoke cleared, all the figures were gone.

***

Wren struggled through coughing fits while the remnants of the tobacco smoke dissipated. After a quick crawl to his water pot, Wren lifted the pot to his lips before gulping down most of the pot's contents. The pot then slipped from his grasp, smashing into pieces as Wren stared to the edge of the firelight to William's area of the lodge. The priest was gone!

Grabbing a lit log from the fire, Wren annihilated the shadows about the lodge until he checked the entire floor; William was nowhere. Breathing heavily, Wren considered what monstrosities the matrons could have unleashed when a cold, stiff breeze parted the hide covering the doorway. A soft groan hung to the high-pitched whine of wind.

"William?" Wren asked aloud as he charged out the lodge's entrance, the log releasing tired embers with every step. Outside, a sliver of Moon pierced through haunting clouds that were casting a soft veil of snow over the landscape. Scanning the village's center, Wren spied a figure writhing on the ground. Snow covered the form, which clumsily moved about without any apparent direction. Then, Moon broke through more of the cloud cover, illuminating the figure as it collapsed, which revealed the interior of the figure's outer garments.

"Black Robe," Wren whispered as he ran to William. Tossing his impromptu torch aside, Wren kneeled down by William's side before gently grasping the priest's shoulder.

"Ah! Careful there," William cried as he winced. Moon's light allowed Wren to see the numerous welts and cuts about the priest's face.

"What happened?" Wren asked, uncertain what to do.

"I told them a joke. Don't think they liked it," William replied before he laughed. He quickly coughed and winced, grabbing at his abdomen while his laughter continued. Wren suddenly laughed along with his friend.

"You Irish are a strange people," he finally said before helping William to his feet and escorting the priest back to the lodge.

Chapter 10

Wren helped William to the ground just by the fire. Then, after pulling furs over to William, Wren helped lower the injured man until William was resting fully on the furs. The young Erie then moved about the lodge gathering the remaining pot of water and several scraps of deerskin to where William lay. All the while, the priest sang.

Will you remember me in time,
Debra Arun…

Will you pray for me o'er the years,
Debra Arun…

My heart, my heart, cries for thee,
Debra Arun…

For we must part whilst in this world,
Debra Arun…

The melody was haunting, William's sorrow familiar, and the moment left Wren speechless. The elders spoke of Black Robes as sorcerers, demons even. *Could a demon sing of pain? Could demons feel as a human did?*

"Who was this woman you cry for?" Wren asked as he wrung the excess water from the skin.

"And here I thought you didn't speak English," William said while looking up through the lodge's ventilation shaft.

"I don't need to know your words to feel your pain. Your voice carries on the air as did mine after Wind's Whisper was taken," Wren replied as he gently wiped at the open wounds on William's face.

"She's the love of my life, as fair as any rainbow or sunrise this world can offer," William said, his eyes never averting from the gap in the roof.

"Where is she?" Wren dared ask after moments of silence passed.

"She's with my family, far beyond my reach, in a place where the English will not find them." William turned and looked at Wren and smiled, though his eyes pooled with tears.

"Can you not join them, friend William?"

"That's in God's hands, Calling Wren, but for as long as I live, as my love and family will never step upon the Emerald Isle again, nor shall I." Wren asked no more of the priest as he dabbed William's wounds with the soaked deerskin.

***

The call of a pair of cardinals woke Wren from his restless sleep. With the sun's rays barely edging the horizon, Wren's eyes struggled to see the lodge's interior. The lodge's fire down to embers, he huddled tightly in his bed of furs until he finally willed himself to toss a couple logs into the firepit. Using a branch as a poker, Wren stirred the embers about until a flame took hold of the new fuel. Wren then crouched near the flames, enjoying the warmth and the nearing sounds of the male and female cardinal calling one another seemingly just outside the lodge. The moment of solace ended abruptly as the sleeping priest snorted, a snort that led into a series of snores.

"What does he keep in that nose?" Wren whispered after struggling to suppress a chuckle. For a time, Wren considered how quickly he befriended William. The circumstances made the friendship possible. That realization disheartened Wren, because he reasoned a Jesuit, a Black Robe, would not be so easily trusted or accepted if Wren were amongst his own people. "What a curious creature we humans are," Wren whispered as he turned back towards the fire.

Soon after the sun's rays negated the need for firelight to see clearly, a throng of Seneca men, bear clan members donning bear fur robes and bear claw necklaces, brought in pots of water and corn soup, enough for both Wren and William. The bear clan members then exited the lodge without uttering a word.

"Will you ever wake?" Wren asked the still sleeping (and snoring) priest as Wren gently patted William on the cheek.

"Let me be, I was having such a lovely dream," William said. The priest then groaned while curling up into a ball under his amassed furs.

"Dream later, eat now," Wren chided as he moved over to the pots of food. "Come, before the food cools." William, famished, still took a bit of time waking, stretching on the ground to loosen his limbs. The first stretch caused considerable pain as the priest's stomach remained sore from the previous evening's beating. Yet, the more he moved about, the more William adjusted to his pain and injuries. Wrapping a large fur around his shoulders, William finally joined Wren as the Erie finished his own pot of soup.

"Soup again?" William asked. Wren nodded as he passed a small pot of corn soup to the priest. William wasted little time digging a wooden spoon into the thick broth stocked with ample corn and beans. Wren, meanwhile, washed his breakfast down with gulps of water. William took a second to watch as Wren again lifted the pot of water to his lips and drank deeply. "That doesn't happen to be whiskey now, does it?" Wren looked quizzically at William while still drinking from the pot.

"Whiskey?" Wren asked after handing the pot of water over to the priest.

"It's a drink, made from fermented grains," he replied before looking at and sniffing the liquid contents. "Certainly not whiskey." William took a sip of water before returning his attention to his soup.

"Is whiskey, good?" Wren asked, curious to learn more of William and the Irish. William, for his part, quickly regretted the mention of the beverage. He already witnessed French and Englishmen giving over rum and brandy, the intent to trade with the natives after their inebriation. William thought for long moments before answering.

"Whiskey, rum, any of the drinks the French and English provide, you should avoid. Drinking them causes your mind to wander."

"Wander?" Wren asked; the priest knew he had said too much already, but the door was open now.

"Rum and whiskey make it hard to focus on your duties. Drink too much, and you're likely to fall asleep or agree to trade away your homes without gaining anything." A glint in Wren's eyes reflected his newfound understanding.

"We make drinks from bark and roots that do the same. Causes terrible head pain the next morning," Wren replied before taking another swig of water. Wren's seeming indifference scared the priest. *Had his Celtic ancestors been so nonchalant about the arrival of the English to Ireland's shores?*

"The English and French have tasted the riches of this New World, your homeland," William said as his visage grew somber. "They will never leave now. You, the Seneca, the Huron, you are all in danger of losing everything; your homes, your families, your lives.

"I know the English. They will think nothing of killing your people in order to posses your land. Withdraw to older hunting grounds, and wait out the diseases and conflict we brought. Return only after the world has calmed and you

have amassed enough defenders to take back
what is rightfully yours."

The priest's words chilled Wren's soul. The
young Erie instantly thought of his father and the
village matrons. *"How do I warn them? Where
will we go?"* His questions ended abruptly as a
contingent of young, Seneca men and an elderly
woman, robed in bearskins, entered the lodge.

"It is time, Featherling," the woman said,
tossing a bear robe to the ground at Calling
Wren's feet.

***

After binding William's hands and feet to a
roof support and Wren donned the offered robe,
the Seneca led Wren outside, the men, clutching
spears, marching behind Wren while the woman
walking at his side into the snow covered village.
The acrid smell of his new fur robe overwhelmed
Wren's senses as they meandered through the
village. As days earlier, Wren was again taken
aback by the variety of longhouse design spread
throughout the village. He also was fascinated
by the onlookers the procession passed. Only
the Bear Clan seemed to be taking part in the
ceremony. As for the other villagers, Wren perceived a variety of emotions felt by the Seneca
residents. The children seemed awed at Wren's
presence, as if the young Erie was a sacred guest

of the Bear Clan. Other villagers, those who appeared fellow adoptees, looked saddened as if they were reliving their own adoption. *Was this a betrayal to the Erie?* Wren shook off the momentary depression; he was given no *real* choice here. Instead, he focused on the Seneca whose eyes reflected anger, an anger Wren believed for the Erie's assaults on the Haudenosaunee.

***

The procession ended at the entrance to a longhouse over whose portal was suspended the jaws of a great bear. The shock of the bear's projected size soon vanished as Wren stepped up to the hide-covered entrance.

"Will Featherling consume me? Is this where Calling Wren ends?" Wren hesitated before entering, wondering how the coming rite would affect him. Then, moving into and beyond the longhouse's end storage area, Wren walked into the dark interior living space where seemingly every Bear Clan member stood. Wren scanned the room's occupants; each face stoic, unmoving.

"Sisters and brothers, daughters and sons, my Featherling has returned!" his female escort proclaimed preempting a wave of cheers through the assembled voices. Wren was then shoved into the embraces of the matrons and other clan members, each introducing herself or himself until finally, Wren faced his female escort.

"Remember me, Featherling," she said as she clasped his hands warmly. Tears welled in her eyes until water flowed over each of her sun-blanched cheeks. "I am your mother, Corin." Corin then embraced Wren as if she would never let go.

"Am I now reborn?" Calling Wren thought as the festivities continued around him. *"Am I now Seneca?"*

In that moment, confusion and fear slipped from the world as a hawk's piercing cry seized Wren's attention. The raptor, perched up upon the nearest roof opening, peered down at Wren, its gaze hypnotic and stern. Time stood still as Wren and the hawk locked gazes. Suddenly, lightning illuminated Sky, and the following thunder rattled the longhouse, which ultimately drew Wren's gaze to the other occupants. Amazingly, none of the Seneca seemed to notice the growing wrath of the coming storm. Their jubilation continuing, unfettered. Wren looked back to the hawk for an explanation, which is when familiarity struck. It was the hawk's eyes, dark beyond the deepest recesses of the night sky. Another lightning bolt lit Sky and cast a haze over the hawk until all but the raptor's talons were a blur. Then as the thunder replied to the its partner, the hawk's form flashed between a feathered monarch of the clouds to the great fish of his waking dreams. Another flash of lightning momentarily blinded Wren. Once his eyes adjusted, Wren looked back and the hawk remained perched above.

"Talon?" Wren asked, now totally oblivious to the surrounding Seneca.

"*Live free, live Erie,*" the bird seemed to call out before vaulting back into the clouds. In the hawk's wake, time moved forward, and Wren felt a part of the throng. Yet, not one of his new family appeared to have witnessed what transpired.

After the fleeting moments of laughter and acceptance, Calling Wren once again felt alone in the midst of the enemy.

Chapter 11

Featherling's mother, Matron Corin, escorted Wren about the Bear Clan longhouse introducing the Erie prisoner as *Featherling*. Wren witnessed adoption ceremonies before, and he knew that silence was the best course of action. The Bear Clan members, one by one, embraced Wren whispering "Welcome back, brother," before releasing their grasp. Then, after passing nearly to the opposite end of the longhouse, Wren encountered Wind's Whisper.

"Welcome back, Beloved," she whispered after embracing Wren tightly. Amidst the raucous celebrants, Whisper's words were lost except to Wren. Her warmth and scent brought a rush of memory and pain, but the moment was fleeting. Whisper moved away fearing someone would notice the bond; she didn't move quick enough. Hidden in the shadows of the longhouse's central area, the clan's senior matron eyed the exchange.

***

"Dance, Featherling!" exclaimed a throng of Bear Clan members as Sun descended beyond the trees. Wren consented to their request, jumping about amidst the clan's people; women and men, young and old. After feasting on deer shanks and corn stew, Wren actually enjoyed the chance to move about, but the celebration soon took an ugly turn. A number of his new "brothers" spent time preparing a dark brew of pulverized leaves and bark, a pungent concoction that left Wren wanting fresh air. As he was escorted towards the pot, he thought of similar drinks his Erie family brewed and the usual reaction tasters had to it. This was part of the purification rite, at least for some. For others, usually the younger males, it was an initiation. The longhouse suddenly silenced.

Wren took an offered cup of the warm drink, uncertain what steps to then take. He caught Whisper's eye, hoping she would provide direction. She simply nodded towards him. In turn, Wren looked about for the Featherling's mother; she stood near the central fire beside the senior matron. He bowed towards them before turning to the brewers. Then, after a quick prayer to Sky, Wren gulped down the beverage. He felt the caffeinated beverage burn down his throat and through his stomach, and everyone heard the gurgling of Wren's innards. Everyone waited

patiently to how long Wren lasted before the inevitable. It was a near record time before the
drink broke Wren to the point where he vomited
a day's worth of meals into the large pot of the
black brew.

"Featherling! Featherling!" The cries continued as Wren regained composure. His new
family started embracing him again. The brewers, meanwhile, removed the despoiled pot while
Featherling's mother gave Wren a cup of water,
which he eagerly drank.

"Welcome home, my dear Featherling," the
short woman said before pulling Wren down and
kissing his forehead. Retreating slowly from her
grasp, Wren saw tears flood from her eyes.

"*I wish I could bring back your son, matron*," Wren thought after Featherling's mother
walked off. Thoughts of his own mother's grief
soon overwhelmed Wren as the gathered celebrants started to return to their own "apart-
ments," the areas where a nuclear family bunked
for the night. Now, Wren would sleep with
Featherling's parents until he wed a woman from
another clan. As Whisper was part of the same
clan now, at least in the eyes of the Seneca, their
marriage was now forbidden for they were considered cousins.

"You look troubled, Featherling," the senior
Bear Clan matron said, snapping Wren from his

torturous thoughts. He knew he would never adjust to his new Seneca name. He would forever remain his parent's son.

"I feel fortunate to have been accepted into the Bear Clan." The stoic matron showed no tells, her mind and intent perfectly hidden.

"Adoption is a difficult process, young one. The portal to the Great Village is now open, but only in time will we know if your mergence with Featherling is complete." The matron's words chilled Wren to his core. *Could she sense his resistance to the adoption?*

"I will seek to aid Featherling's return, matron," Wren said, hoping to appease the head of his new family. The matron smirked before stretching her hand out to Wren.

"Walk with me, young one," she said, a curious smirk briefly breaking the matron's stolid stance. Wren took her hand where upon she led him outside the longhouse, into the frigid night air. Above, Moon cast a sliver of light through a patchwork of clouds and stars. The matron ended their trek within the light of Moon's nearest beam. There in silence they stood for a time while the cool air chilled their skin and seared through their lungs. Wren wanted to run back into the warmth of the longhouse, but he knew not to leave the matron's side.

The village itself rested. Aside from plumes of smoke venting from the collected longhouses, no movement was visible. Even the two guards posted alone the palisade remained motionless, like trees guarding the entrance to a forest.

"This is my favorite time of day," the matron said, her gaze cast to Moon and the stars beyond. "All is quiet, peaceful, and few sounds ever arise to challenge the silence. Now is when life is most potent."

"It is indeed beautiful, matron," Wren said, though his mind actually did nothing else but replay the memory of Whisper's embrace.

"There is but one threat remaining to our village's harmony, and I need your help to combat it," the matron said never turning her gaze from Moon.

"The white-kin, matron?" Wren asked as he turned to her.

"One of the white-kin in particular. The Black Robe I fear may cast spells on us. The Onondaga's Spirit-Guide advised us this morning to thwart the Black Robe before he spins his magic."

"Matron, I think the Black Robe is…"

"You opinion is not being sought, Featherling!" the matron scolded after her head turned, her ominous eyes burning with anger. "You will act on my word!" she commanded.

"The Onondaga's Spirit-Guide advised we remove the fingers and tongue of the Black Robe immediately and then sacrifice him. I now agree this must be done, and I order you to do it."

"Matron, I mean no disrespect, but I…"

"Again, you speak without reason, Featherling. The Black Robe has already impacted your mind, which you do not see, yet. Tomorrow, as Sun rises, you will take the Black Robe out to the woods, and after having this sorcerer chop wood to replace what he used, you will take his fingers." She then pulled a necklace from beneath her robe, literally a strap adorned with charred fingers. "This man threatens our people so you will stop him." The matron saw the conflict in Wren's eyes, and she immediately moved to assure her Will would be followed. "Return tomorrow with the Black Robe's fingers, else I will reason that you and Wind's Whisper are our enemies as well." Wren looked into the matron's gaze and knew the implications of her words, particularly her use of Whisper's true name. He had no choice.

"Come, my dear Featherling," the matron said, her tone now tender. "It has become cool. Let us return to the warmth of our home."

Chapter 12

Wren's first evening in the longhouse afforded little rest or comfort. Taking Featherling's place, Wren slept on the longhouse bench where Featherling's parents and sister slept. Sharing a large bearskin blanket, the four huddled to keep warm. The scent of the well-fueled fire pits along with the distant sounds of wind racing through gaps in the longhouse's structure sparked memories of his own home amongst the Erie. Yet, huddled with strangers, he constantly felt out of place, threatened, as if he would be cast out, seen as an invader. That feeling alone made sleep difficult, but other concerns generated even more terror.

"Torture my friend or risk Whisper's life," Wren constantly thought even though there was no question as to his future actions. William, an acquaintance of but a couple days, had become a trusted friend. Yet, he was of the white-kin. *Could the Black Robe be truly trusted? Was William already spinning webs of deceit over the Iroquoians?* Wren's heart quickly disavowed

those thoughts. William was a friend, which made his coming actions all the more painful.

Sleep finally conquered Wren's anxiety near morning, but with it came painful visions. Again, Erie villages burned as his family and kin fled to the woodlands, a host of Seneca, Onondaga and English in pursuit. Wren was there, fleeing with his family, but his escape was short-lived. A musket slammed into Wren's right shoulder blade, driving him into the ground. When he turned over, the Seneca who bore Talon stood overhead, smiling. The Seneca then raised his firearm, the barrel aimed at Wren's head. The Seneca pulled the trigger...

The vision ended abruptly, replaced by peaceful blue skies covering a vast body of water. Again, he tasted the salt intermixed with the mist, and again the voice came.

"I am here, Calling Wren," the great fish said as it vaulted from the water. "You are not alone." The vision brought Wren comfort, strength and peace.

***

Warmer air welcomed the morning and the Seneca, as did Sky, now cleared of all traces of clouds. Wren, after eating bits of dried deer meat, left the longhouse to stroll towards the lodge where William slept. Wren, draped in a bearskin cloak, walked slowly, chilled by what he must do and enthralled by the freedom he now had within the village.

The lone lodge in the village, it was easy to pinpoint where William rested, but getting to the lodge proved easier than entering.

"Talon, give me guidance," Wren prayed as he reached for the hide covering the lodge's entryway. To Wren's periphery, hidden behind a pile of firewood, stood the Seneca possessing Talon, Wren's beloved charm. Wren kept his eyes to the hide before him while remembering William's words of caution; this Seneca was not to be trusted and to be avoided. For now, Wren could do nothing, but he determined to remain guarded whenever the Seneca drew near. Refocusing on more pressing issues, Wren entered the lodge.

Darkness reined inside the lodge as no fire burned in the pit. Wren darted towards William, the priest huddled around the post to which the Seneca bond him. With only his cloak for warmth, William shivered violently,

"William!" Wren exclaimed as he embraced the priest hoping to warm his friend with his own body heat. "You're going to be all right, my friend."

"You haven't happened to see my hands and feet, have you? William joked.

"How does he hold on?" Wren thought as he wrapped the priest in his cloak before gathering the furs placed just out of William's reach. He then wrapped the assorted furs around William before lighting a fire. After a blaze stabilized, Wren helped William over to the fire. Feeling soon returned to William's extremities at which time Wren was able leave to secure soup corn bread and a few bits of dried venison from the Bear Clan's longhouse. Wren wanted to stay with the priest, but only the Bear Clan would give Wren food. The two shared the meal, remaining silent while both considered the coming day.

"What happened here?" Wren asked after William seemed warm and on the mend. The priest smiled.

"I think I may have worn out my welcome." William laughed as he considered the events Wren missed. "After they took you, they took the furs and poured water over the fire. They said I should ask my God for fire."

"Did you?" Wren immediately regretted his question. Yet, if William was irked by it, the priest showed no sign of anger or frustration.

"The Lord knows what I need to do His bidding. If I needed fire for His purpose, then this dwelling would blaze with unquenchable flames." William's voice became stern yet graceful. "Challenge not the Lord, nor make demands of the Creator. He provides in His own time."

"I'm sorry if I offended you, Black Robe."

"Black Robe? I thought we were passed that, Calling Wren?" William's humor surfaced once more, erasing the moment of strain between them. "You and I have different beliefs. That doesn't mean we can't be friends." Wren smiled and nodded towards William, uncertain what to say. William was not so at a loss for words.

"So, Calling Wren, are you here to kill me?" Wren felt his jaws lock and a shiver run up his spine. He long considered an answer to William's query. Honesty seemed the only appropriate manner in which to proceed.

"Not to kill, but to…" Wren struggled to find his voice.

"Cut out my eyes or ears?" William said with a smile, his nonchalance unnerving.

"Your fingers, all of them, but only after you spend the day chopping wood to replace that which you've used."

"I see," William said as he looked down into the small pot of soup he was eating from. Wren watched the Black Robe swish around the remaining broth, corn and beans with a wooden spoon, his visage reflecting calm and acceptance.

"Do you have anymore of the cornbread?" William asked, breaking the silence and Wren's resolve in one instant.

"Are you mad!" Wren exclaimed throwing his pot into the dirt. The vessel shattered, releasing the remaining soup over the compacted earth.

"A pity that, wasting a good soup," William said as he returned his attention to his own pot. Exasperated, Wren simply looked down at the sitting priest who seemed so irrationally composed. Wren then laughed as a bit of understanding crept into his soul.

"It was a good soup wasn't it?" Wren commented as he sat down by the fire. "How did you know?"

"You're traveling amongst your enemy without a guard. I simply reasoned a deal was struck; you torture me or they torture Whisper. Am I right?" Wren nodded in response. William stood and walked over by Wren, taking a seat next to the young Erie. "When I was assigned to this land, I was informed of the dangers that previous priests had encountered. I came here fully aware of what might happen, and truthfully, I was expecting to die." Wren shot a look of astonishment at the priest. *Maybe he was mad!*

"I came here wanting to help others find comfort in this world," William continued, his eyes now cast deep into the fire. "The pain of my loss replaced by the joy of others, helping others follow their dreams? That became my purpose, my reason for living. I will die knowing I did what I could for others and knowing that soon I shall be with my family." The priest turned to face Wren once more, and in William's eyes Wren saw the depth of his friend's despair as well as the hope in his sacrifice. They both smiled.

"Come on now," William said, patting Wren on the back. "We've got some wood to gather."

***

"I'm surprised you weren't commanded to kill me, to be honest," William commented as he wrestled a branch the size of his leg from under the undulating drifts of snow. They were making their second trip beyond the palisade along the snow-covered ground, collecting fallen limbs to replace the wood William and Wren used during their time amongst the Seneca.

"The matrons will oversee your execution, and all the village will participate," Wren replied, saddened by the fate awaiting William. *Should he inform the priest of what was to come?*

"Such despair all for me?" William asked, snapping Wren back to his senses. The two men stopped walking and faced each other, William seemingly contented while Wren was disheartened. "Let me guess," William continued. "They will break the bones in my hands and limbs before stripping flesh from my body. Then, over the course of the night, the villagers will take turns poking me with sticks fresh from a fire. Finally, when sunlight pierces the Heavens, they will cut off my head and pull out my heart, not necessarily in that order. Does that sum up what is to come?"

"How did you, I mean…"

"Reports from other Jesuits detailed such ceremonies amongst the Huron, I mean Wendat." Wren nodded and smiled briefly at the priest's use of the true name of the Erie's ally to the north. Without another word, the two men looked north. There, beyond a growing mist, they saw a lone pine reaching high above all else. Both men ceased movement to gaze at the elder tree, but each saw something different amidst the branches, needles and cones. Wren's vision spied his grandfather, dead nearly five years now. Proud and strong, Wren's grandfather was one of the great keepers of Erie tradition who taught Wren about the origins of the Erie and their victories over and defeats to enemies, the forests and the demons that dwelled just beyond the reaches of Erie territory. For a moment, Wren's heart filled with joy as the calls of cardinals, chickadees and downy woodpeckers chipped away at his feelings of loss.

William's vision saw the Holy Spirit embedded within the pine's branches. One moment, William saw The Crucifix, a sight that instantly rekindled his faith in his mission to the New World, even if it meant his death. Then, as seconds passed, the tree's branches, needles and cones morphed into an image that reminded the priest of Mary holding the newborn Christ while they escaped with Joseph beyond the grasp of their enemies. It was in those seconds that the growing mist darkened, blurring all else about the landscape. For Wren and William, the visions, though different in image, signified the same thing. Intruders were coming.

Chapter 13

"An Enemy," both men whispered simultaneously as the birdsongs of the forest suddenly
silenced. From their position just beyond the
stout palisade, Wren and William heard the
movement of branches and the trouncing of
snow and dried leaves.

"Erie?" William asked as they lowered their
bundles of wood to the ground. Wren shook his
head.

"My people would not be so loud." Wren
scanned the length of the nearby sections of the
village's palisade until he spotted a Seneca
guard; the guard was slumped over the palisade's
rampart, an arrow embedded in his head. Farther
down the palisade, towards the main gate, Wren
observed a score of men running unchecked towards the village entrance. "Invaders!" Wren
cried as he ran to the nearest stretch of the palisade, which stood over twice his height. William
was there before Wren could even call for help.
The priest squatted down allowing Wren to stand
on his shoulders. William stood with difficulty,

permitting Wren to grab hold of the palisades upper limits.

"Invaders!" Wren cried again as he heaved himself over the wall. Without looking to William, he ran along the parapet to the nearest ladder down. Already Wren could hear cries from the villagers and attackers alike, all of whom were on the opposite side of the village.

**

William Sullivan darted off towards the village's entrance immediately after Wren climbed over the palisade. Halting momentarily to pick up a sapling from a stout pile used for longhouse repairs, William heard Wren's cries of alarm. The village had been warned! Yet, the cries of women and children, and his memory of previous massacres, propelled the priest forward. Staff in hand, an old instinct took control.

For the Seneca and the attackers, seeing the Black Robe charge through the gate and into the fray seemed surreal. *Black Robes were not fighters!* If the English or Romans had been present, they would have viewed William's assault quite differently, recognizing the Irishman for what he truly was; *a Celt!*

"Deus vult (God wills it)!" Father William Sullivan cried, the voice of a thousand crusaders channeling through his heart, lungs and vocal cords. His presence honorably announced, William attacked the nearest invader who wore a beaver-fur cloak over deerskin shirt and leggings. The young invader's face was a shocking sight, his face covered in tattoo lines and a silver ring pierced through the man's septum. William pushed aside the invader's head and focused on reality; defend or die!

William slammed his impromptu staff down on the invader's shaved head, rendering the invader unconscious, but fracturing William's weapon in the process. Another invader immediately set upon William in retaliation. Prepared for the priest's coming attack, the older, club-wielding invader was ready and quickly disarmed the priest after William lunged at him. Now weaponless, William shoulder-rushed the invader, but his effort proved fruitless. The slightly shorter but stronger-built invader simply brought up his knee into William's face; the priest collapsed, dazed and unprotected. The invader stood above the priest, his club raised to strike the killing blow, but the club never fell.

"Eriehronon!" Wren cried out as he ran towards the combatants, notched bow in hand. Stopping and drawing the bow full, Wren let his arrow fly just as William's attacker's club began its descent; the arrow pierced through the invader's back and heart, the force knocking the dead man on top of William. All the gathered, invaders and villagers, locked eyes on the Erie, Wren's battle cry silencing all else. For a long moment, Wren scanned the event's players, assessing the greatest need. An elder matron, held to the ground by one of the invaders, looked to Wren, her pale eyes pleading for intervention. Wren answered.

"Sky, guide my aim!" Wren exclaimed as he cast another arrow into the wind. The projectile found its mark in the invader's neck; the matron was safe. Then, in rapid succession, Wren cast four more arrows pulled from a quiver slung over his shoulder. Each projectile flew with critical accuracy, felling four more invaders. The three remaining invaders fled while Seneca defenders finished off the injured enemy with club, axe and arrow. Wren now looked to the priest who struggled under the weight of the dead invader. Pulling at the fallen invader's arm left William a manageable weight to push off."

"What kept you?" William asked as Wren pulled the priest to his feet. William, saturated in blood, was breathing heavily, but still donning the smile Wren was now accustomed to.

"Irish," Wren mumbled as he clasped William's forearm and smiled. The two men then shared a brief laugh before taking in the carnage about them. The attack cost the invaders dearly as only three escaped, and Seneca defenders were in pursuit; the three would not escape. For the Seneca, six men, women and children, old and young, fell to clubs and arrows. Another five were critically injured.

"I'll see to the wounded," William said, but Wren quickly grasped the priest's upper arm preventing William from moving forward. Five archers stood within twenty paces of the Erie and the Black Robe, and all five had an arrow readied. Wren released his grip from his friend before tossing his bow and quiver to the ground. Both Wren and William awaited their deaths.

"Enough!" cried out the Bear Clan matron as she trudged through the wet snow towards Wren and William. Stopping within ten paces, the matron smirked before nodding to each in turn. "Let them be," she then said at which time the archers lowered their bows. The matron then scanned those present, noting fear, anger and sorrow in looks of her family and friends. "See to the wounded," the matron commanded in a motherly tone before she moved up to the Black Robe.

"I am told that your kind have healing powers. Is this so?" she asked cordially.

"I have no magical abilities, if that is what you mean, but I am skilled at bandaging wounds and using herbs to help injuries heal," William replied. "I would be happy to assist your people."

"You would have my gratitude for helping, Black Robe." She then turned to Wren, troubled by the young man's choice of battle cry. *Would he ever become one of them?* "Featherling! See to the Black Robe's needs." At the matron's command, Wren nodded while all the villagers accepted the matron's wishes. Wren and the Black Robe would live, for now.

***

The seriously injured were carried to the lodge where William and three elder matrons administered aid. After cleaning the assorted lacerations and bruises, William and the matrons applied a poultice of herbs and mashed pumpkin. The poultice, first diluted and warmed in a pot set in the fire pit ashes, would help with the swelling and controlling infection. However, the assembled caretakers knew the remedy mattered little if they failed to stop wounds from bleeding. Consequently, William and the matrons needed to constantly assess each of the injured.

At first, none of the Seneca permitted Father William to treat them. *Is he not an evil sorcerer?* Fortunately, once the clan matrons took turns holding an injured Seneca's hand during William's treatments, all fears subsided.

"May God bless and heal you," Father William continually prayed in silence, not wanting to offend his captors nor frighten the injured as he tended to his patients. The priest worked without rest, constantly assuring the fur and linen bandages he made still held. As for the injured, Father William also never left a patient without first speaking a word or two of encouragement. His kindness helped further ease the situation.

To help, Wren ran about the village gathering scraps of fur and linen from every longhouse while clans took turns fueling the lodge's fire and refilling the large pots of water and corn soup set in the ashes of the structure's lone fire pit. In between such errands, Wren watched, amazed that the Black Robe could be so gentle to the very people who threatened to cut off his fingers. Outside, in the growing dark, the Bear Clan matron wondered at the same thing.

"What is this man?" she whispered, watching Father William's actions through a gap in the furs covering the lodge's entrance. Sunset now passed, the matron huddled into her bearskin robe enduring the winter chill in order to remain hidden from the Black Robe's gaze. Contented by her observations, the matron walked off towards her clan's longhouse. With temperatures beyond bitter, the matron's footfalls preceded a muffled crunch with every step, which silenced only when she stopped her walk at the long-house's entrance. Once there, she turned to peer up at the stars and half-moon that lit her way.

"Can the white-kin truly show compassion?" she asked, wondering if the Oki would ever respond to her. After a few more breaths of the cold air, the matron entered the longhouse to consider her choices.

***

"The Onondaga warned us before they left," Rising Sun said as he meandered about the other villagers gathered in the Turtle Clan's longhouse. One of the younger Seneca fighters, Rising Sun received the attention from the elders only because of his mother's status as the Turtle Clan's senior matron. He intended to usurp every moment of the impromptu conference to silence a threat while seeking revenge for the love that betrayed him.

"This Erie will ever be our enemy!" Rising Sun exclaimed, ripping the neclace from his neck, which bore Wren's shark tooth. "He bears charms, bits from monsters of the abyss," he said holding up the shark tooth aloft so the gathered could see. "Only one of the Windigo's spawn would carry such a charm!" Rising Sun's voice reverberated throughout the longhouse stirring even the slumbering children and infirm.

A sudden alertness came to Rising Sun as all the clan's members stood and bowed their heads. Aside from the crackle of the fires, all Rising Sun now heard was the shuffle of feet behind him.

"Would spawn of the Windigo defend the Seneca as this Erie did?" an all too familiar voice asked. Rising Sun turned to see the senior matrons surrounding Lopi, whom he married shortly after her capture; at the front of the enclave stood Lopi's adopted mother, the bear clan's senior matron. Rising Sun quickly bowed his head, though his frame remained relaxed, indifferent. "You continue to set free venom amongst our people, Rising Sun. Have you learned nothing?" the bear clan matron continued. "You spew hatred and malcontent everywhere. Hiawatha himself would struggle to pacify your heart. You shame your clan, the Seneca and the Three Sisters! You are an apparition drawn from the recesses of Tadadaho's mind before the Peace Maker soothed his soul."

"Matron Reese, I..."

"Be silent, Rising Sun!" the Bear Clan matron exclaimed, ending Rising Sun's rebuke abruptly. "You lost all right to invoke my name when you brought violence to my daughter, Lopi, and violence to my house."

"She is Erie, matron," Rising Sun interjected. "She will always be Erie. Call her Lopi all you wish, for she will ever remain 'Wind's Whisper' in her own heart."

A deluge of water smacked Rising Sun's head. Shaking off the cold wash, Rising Sun snapped his head in the direction from which the water originated. There, set with a cold gaze, eyes flared in anger, stood Rising Sun's mother, Matron Verell. As tall as most of the village's men, Matron Verell looked imposing as she stared at her son while grasping a head-sized clay vessel that moments earlier held water.

"How does a son of mine not know his place?" his mother asked as she smashed the water pot at Rising Sun's feet. The longhouse occupants stared in silence, all awaiting for Rising Sun to accept his failure.

"I apologize, matrons," Rising Sun said as he turned and bowed to his mother and the other matrons of his clan. He then, begrudgingly bowed to Matron Reese. "I also apologize to you, matron. I beg your forgiveness."

"Perhaps some day you will have it, Rising Sun," Matron Reese replied before turning to face Matron Verell. "Mind you this, Turtle Clan, such belligerence could cost us dearly. "I understand your apprehension at the Black Robe's presence. Yet, we cannot dismiss this white-kin's assistance during and after the fight. We dare not risk insulting the Three Sisters by executing a white-kin the Three may have sent.

"And what if this Black Robe is a servant of evil, purposed with destroying us?" Rising Sun's mother retorted. Matron Reese approached the Turtle Clan matron and bowed, slightly, after stopping feet from her long-time nemesis.

"React not to the anxiety of your son, dear sister. Men are impetuous, often acting without forethought. Do you truly believe I would act so carelessly?" Matron Reese asked.

"Then what do you propose we do?" Matron Verell asked, her gaze frozen by distain.

"I have decided to turn over the Black Robe to the English when they arrive," Matron Reese said turning to stare at the matrons amongst her audience. "Let them risk offending the greater powers." Nods of agreement spread throughout the gathered even as Matron Reese turned her back to Rising Sun's mother and exited the Turtle Clan's longhouse.

Chapter 14

Father William Sullivan, far from his home on the shores of the Emerald Isle, sprinted about the Seneca lodge to administer all possible aid to those injured in the attack. Now hours after the attack, William and the gathered Seneca 'healers' were concentrating efforts on the most severely injured. The two gravest of the injured, an elderly man and a young girl, who appeared no more than ten, were entrusted to the priest. William, ever vigilant, continuously changed his patients' bandages and offered words of comfort whenever the two regained consciousness. Now hours passed nightfall, William's strength ebbed while his heart throbbed with grief. He knew one of the patient's under his care would not last the night.

In an attempt to find some strength and solace, William took a cup of cool water from a large ceramic container. After drawing several sips from the wooden cup, the priest emptied the remaining water over his brow. Then, sitting close to the fire, William closed his eyes and listened to the crackling fire. With only the occasional howl from the wind, William sat undisturbed while memories of his parents, siblings and others now gone emerged. His eyes still shut, the drying beads of water upon his brow were replaced by tears as sorrow soon replaced his solace.

"Tears for me, Black Robe?" asked the man under William's care. William opened his eyes and looked at his charge; the man was smiling, a smile William returned.

"Just thinking of home," William replied before standing and walking over to the man's side. The priest knelt next to the mat, which his elderly patient rested on. "Can I get you anything?" William asked hoping he could in some way make the man comfortable.

"You've done enough for us already, young one. Please, take a rest for a moment." William sat back, grateful for the moment to rest. The elder's smile, meanwhile, disappeared as his gaze focused on the girl resting nearby. "Will my granddaughter recover, Black Robe?"

"She is already on the mend, worry not," William replied as he rested his hand on the man's shoulder. "She has great strength."

"She gets that from her grandmother," the elder replied as his smile returned. A bit of quiet laughter passed between them before seriousness of the attack returned. "Do they know who was behind the attack?"

"I heard talk of the Mississaugas, but no one has yet told me for certain," William replied. The elder simply nodded in response, which left William wondering if the elder was not surprised of the attackers' identity or the fact that the priest was not confided in as to the identity of the perpetrators. A sudden coughing fit from the man's granddaughter distracted both. Rushing to her side, William gently elevated the girl's head until her cough subsided. The priest then placed a balled up robe under the girl's head and neck to keep her torso elevated. All the while, her grandfather looked on, contented that the priest would make her well.

"Rest now, young one," William said as he covered the girl with an additional blanket. He then moved back to the girl's grandfather to continue their talk, but he was too late. The grandfather had passed on.

**

Wren returned from collecting supplies not long after the elder passed. The matrons, with William's help, had moved the man's remains outside onto a scaffold. There, in the rising winds, the fur wrapped body rested amid a cold, star-filled sky. In the lodge, the attending matrons and remaining injured slept. Darting about, Wren tried to find William, but the priest was nowhere to be found. *Was the priest blamed for the elder's death? Had William been executed?*

Heralded by a shrill cry, a stiff wind coursed through the lodge, stirring the hide covering the far entrance. Between the flapping fur, Wren saw William standing in the evening lights. His worries eased, Wren maneuvered through the lodge until he was again out in the frigid air standing next to William.

"I never even knew his name," William said, his eyes never breaking their fixation on the full moon above.

"His name is Feldmer," Wren said as he turned to look at William's face; the priest's cheeks were tear-soaked and eyes reddened. The priest's eyes remained fixed on Moon, an occasional blink William's only visible movement until the call of a cardinal pierced the silence. The bird flew into sight and landed on the palisade.

"Good morning, Da," William said as the first rays of sunlight pierced the veil of night. For the first time in hours, William truly felt at peace and smiled.

"Da?"

"It's what I called my father."

"Your father is a bird?" Wren asked amidst a flurry of chuckles. The two men turned towards each other and laughed harder before returning their attention to the bird.

"My father used to sit outside our home and whistle to the birds," William said as he thought longingly about times spent watching his father sing and whistle. "At some point, a red bird, similar to that one, landed on a maple near Da and whistled back. For years it seemed that bird would come out at night to whistle with my father. Now, whenever I see a red bird, I think it's my father coming to check in on me."

"Your father is a great whistler," Wren said before they both started laughing again.

"What about you? Why did your parents name you Calling Wren?"

"When my mother was in labor, a wren flew into the rafters of the longhouse and chirped as my mother cried out. My father tried everything to chase the bird away, but it wouldn't leave. Then, after I was born, the wren supposedly chirped as if in response to my wails."

"Calling Wren," William said as he returned his gaze to the cardinal.

"Calling Wren," Wren repeated, glorifying in his name and his true self. "Live free, live Erie."

"And what of Featherling?" Matron Reese asked. Both men jumped in surprise, the matron having approached without a sound.

"Matron," Wren and William said simultaneously as they both bowed to the Bear Clan's leading matron, wondering if their conversation would lead to their immediate execution. The matron remained silent as she glanced up at Moon as if looking for direction.

"Long have our peoples lived here, Calling Wren," she said, her use of Wren's true name, a cue both men noticed with alarm. "Tell me, would your Erie mother approve of your current actions?" she asked now standing face to face with Wren. "How many Seneca and Wendat have the Erie adopted? Are they not expected to adapt, to accept the Erie way? You have been allowed your life, do you not owe us?" She did not wait for Wren to answer, but instead moved to face the Jesuit. "And you, Black Robe? Without doubt we owe you thanks for your efforts in defending and healing us. Yet, have not your kin caused much grief here? Do you not owe me and the Seneca something?" Neither man spoke, awaiting the matron's permission first. There, under stars, Moon and Sky, silence reined while Matron Reese passed judgment as was her right alone.

"Your silence speaks well for you both," she finally said as she backed up several steps so she could eye them both. "Your acceptance will come in time, Calling Wren, as will your absolute abeyance. And you, Black Robe, your freedom is too much for me to risk."

"But matron," Wren blurted out fearing his friend's death.

"Silence, Featherling!" she exclaimed, her face cold and threatening. Wren immediately ended his tirade and looked to the ground, the fate of Wind's Whisper still his chief concern.

"Well Black Robe," she continued, "will you not speak up for your life." Finally, William lifted his eyes to meet with the matron's. Gone was the quiet priest, the scholar, the pacifist. All that seemed left was the Celt, free of hindrance and distress.

"I am William, son of Edward and Maureen of the Sullivan Clan. Do as you will, matron, but know that your decision is without meaning. My fate is preordained and ultimately the choice of God. You are but an instrument through which his decisions flow. Slay me, for I am ready to meet the Almighty Father." Father William, without bowing, walked forward until he stood but inches from Matron Reese.

"Such insolence," she replied without averting her eyes. "Your fate is in my hands, and I have chosen to ignore the Onondaga and hand you over to the English. Another contingent of Onondaga and English are wintering at a nearby village, and they should be here within the week. I'm sure your fellow white-kin will know of a suitable way to chastise you." Any respect for William Matron Reese held now gone, she sought to isolate the Black Robe to prevent any sedition. "Featherling! Take this white-kin to the lodge and bind him to a support. If he escapes, I will question whether you and Lopi will ever become Seneca." With those last words she turned to Wren, her eyes now laced with anger. "Make no mistake, Featherling. Fail me and I will act swiftly to end your treachery." Without another word, the matron departed leaving the two friends alone to contemplate the Bear Clan's judgment.

Chapter 15

"I can no longer help you, William," Wren said as he bound the priest's wrists to one of the lodge's central support beams. "I can't risk Whisper being handed over to the Onondaga." Wren burned with hate at the decision forced upon him. He knew he must choose between his beloved and his friend; there was never really a choice.

"Why do the Onondaga hate you so?" William asked. For a moment, Wren stopped fidgeting with the fiber cordage he was using to bind the priest. A rush of memories, history and myth weighed on Wren as he contemplated the question.

"When the great Peace Maker presented our mothers with The Truce, it was made clear that we would be a younger brother to the Seneca, Mohawk and Onondaga nations. It is said that the Seneca and Mohawk were keen to our becoming one of the elder brothers, given our prowess in battle, but the Onondaga's chief, Tadadaho, would not share power with another nation.   Not even Hiawatha could persuade Tadadaho, which is when our senior clan matrons rebuked the Haudenosaunee, Tadadaho specifically.   Ever since, the Onondaga have sought to eradicate us.   I have heard that unlike the other peoples subdued by the Haudenosaunee, the Onondaga will not adopt any captured Erie.   Far as I know, only the Seneca have gone against Tadadaho's wishes."

"Is there no chance for you to make peace with the Seneca?" William asked, trying to find a way for Wren's people to be saved, protected.

"We recently killed a contingent of invading Onondaga, which included one of their chiefs. They will never accept peace now, and the Onondaga will push the other Haudenosaunee members towards war.   Either the Haudenosaunee survives or we do."   Wren's voice had grown more somber with each word.

"Your people will survive, Wren," William finally said after a time of silence passed, his jovial spirit as strong as ever.   A ray of sunlight, which broke through the canopy of evergreens and proclaimed the morning's arrival, immediately followed the priest's words.   Wren felt hope, if only for a moment.   He dared flash a smile to William before testing the bindings one last time.   Wren then watched the lodge occupants move about as if it were simply another day. No one questioned the Black Robe's binding, as if William's valiant actions never happened. Wren had never felt so far from home in that moment.

"I will bring you water and food later," Wren said before standing to leave, fearful that taking too long would draw the ire of Matron Reese.

"Wren?" William called out, as Wren moved towards the nearest portal. Wren stopped, his back to the priest, awaiting a curse or rebuke from the friend he was betraying. "Do what you must to save Whisper and yourself. Live, for me and your people." Wren turned towards William, aghast at his friend's words. *Did William not understand he was to die?* As if in response, William smiled and winked. In that moment, Wren knew his friend accepted death as the only way to save Whisper and Wren. The ultimate sacrifice for an Erie the priest just met. His eyes welling with tears, Wren smiled and bowed towards his friend before departing for the Bear Clan's longhouse.

***

Every step towards the longhouse drained a little more of Wren's remaining strength. After a night of running between longhouses, seeking supplies, Wren was exhausted. Now, as he grappled with the thought of fully assuming the role of Featherling, Wren eagerly sought his space on the bench where he could regain his energy and his wits. His effort to seek rest was soon thwarted.

Stepping quickly through the storage area of the Bear Clan longhouse, Wren moved into the interior dwelling space and into the arms of his new extended family.

"FEATHERLING!" the host of Bear Clan members shouted in unison as Wren passed through the bear hide that covered the portal. Soon he was embraced by the clan's males, young and old, each slapping Wren on the back and offering words of cheer for Wren's effort in the battle and in assisting the healers. After Wren passed through the assembled defenders, he found himself standing before the Bear Clan's matrons. Whisper was there, a few yards away. He wanted desperately to hold her, to look into her eyes until sleep took hold, but he knew such attentiveness assumed great risk. Instead, with great difficulty, Wren shifted his gaze to Matron Corin, Featherling's mother, and moved quickly to embrace her.

"I am here... mother," he said, his tone conciliatory.

"It is good that you are home, my son," she replied, pulling back to look up into Wren's eyes. Her smile was void of malice and deceit; it reflected only the love of a mother. "Come, you've had a long night and should rest." Voices of dissent echoed through the dwelling as calls for celebration spread quickly. "Time for jubilation will come," Matron Corin said. "Let the moment's champion have his rest." Without another word, she escorted Wren to their length of bench. Placing a log on the nearest fire pit, Matron Corin then covered Wren with furs as he laid upon the bench. "It is so good that you are home, Featherling," she said before kissing his forehead and leaving Wren. Sleep took hold soon after.

***

The nightmare came quickly and consumed Wren's remaining strength so that all he could do was watch the imagined events unfold. The ever-familiar setting, the Erie village, seemed veiled by smoke. Wren walked closer, climbing the steep hill coming from the creek. Villagers, fleeing from the palisade, ran through Wren, as if he were an unseen apparition. Turning about, Wren suddenly realized that not a sound emanated from the villagers or the surrounding woodlands until a shrill cry sounded from just beyond a section of palisade that stood fifty feet away from him. Seconds later, his mother pushed through a gap in the palisade, the gap forged by the falls of what must have been a thousand falls of metal axe blades. His mother cried out once again as she fled towards him. Wren held out his arms for her, hoping to calm her and determine the source of her grief. He was too late. The Seneca, Rising Sun, emerged from the gap in the palisade and aimed a fire-arm towards Matron Sulvas.

"No!" Wren exclaimed as his mother drew within feet of his position. The firearm exploded, its vaulted projectile slamming into Matron Sulvas's back. The force of the musket ball flung her forward into Wren's waiting arms; she passed right through Calling Wren while, in the distance, Rising Sun smiled with content. Then all turned dark. For long moments, Wren called out to his mother, but no voice returned his cries. He moved around in an attempt to find his footing and direction. His hand touched cold, wet stone. He moved along what felt like a corridor in a cavern, though the edges were smooth. Wren envisioned he was in a tunnel shaped like a longhouse. Time passed until he heard a dripping of water in the distance. As he moved along farther, iridescent ores with the walls provided light. Indeed, the angular cavern was much like a longhouse, though no benches or fire pits or storage areas were visible. Again Wren proceeded, the light intensifying with every step.

"Are you lost?" a melodic voice asked from behind him. Wren spun about and into a defensive posture, his fist raised before his chest. Before him stood a woman who appeared as if she had endured a few more years than Wren. Her hair, long and dark brown, bore a few long white strands, which seemed at odds with her youthful visage and vibrant, blue eyes.

"Matron," Wren finally said after his shock dissipated. He bowed reverently, as if his maternal grandmother stood before him. She bowed in turn, acknowledging the respect Wren showed. Clad in a deerskin cloak, her subtle movement revealed she wore no undergarments. In the instant of revelation, Wren thought he saw a gash over the matron's abdomen. He closed his eyes and bowed once more hoping his errant eyes did not anger the woman.

"Who are you, young one?" she asked.

"I am Wren, matron," he answered. For some reason, he felt as if she should already know him.

"Are you certain? Are you sure you don't answer to another name, because 'Wren' seems out of place." *Had he truly changed? Was he now Seneca?*

"Featherling, matron. That is my new name," Wren answered, bowing again.

"That is definitely not your name, young one. Are you so lost that you have forgotten your true self?"

Wren, truly perplexed, struggled to think of a name that would satisfy the matron. Thoughts of William suddenly flooded his memory. Wren awed at the priest's resolve in sharing his name with Matron Reese and not pleading for his life. Wren's strength returned.

"I am Calling Wren, son of Matron Sulvas of the Deer Clan, from an Erie village a day's journey south of Thunder Falls." The matron smiled.

"Now that I truly believe, Calling Wren. Never hide from your true self for it is the only thing that is truly ever yours." The matron then stepped forward, cupped Wren's face in her hands, and pulled his forehead to her lips. She smelled like the purple bee balm plants found along creeks in spaces where Sun shone brightly all day. As the matron leaned away from Wren, a feeling of loss coursed through him.

"He is ready," she then said. "Again I leave him to you, dear friend." Without another word, she raised her left arm, an action that fully exposed the scars on her abdomen. *Was she injured during childbirth?* The sudden appearance of a hawk, which landed on her arm, distracted Wren from any further contemplation of the matron's wounds.

"I will lead him as best I can, matron," a voice said, which emanated from the hawk that looked quite familiar. For an instant, the hawk appeared to morph into the great fish that visited Wren's recent dreams.

"Talon?" Wren asked as the fish transformed back to its hawk form.

"It is time to return to your journey, Calling Wren," Talon said. The bird then leaped into flight directly towards Wren's head. The young Erie shielded his eyes with his left forearm as Talon drew within a few feet. A moment later, Wren, covered in sweat, was back in the Bear Clan longhouse, his Seneca family sleeping beside him on the bench.

Chapter 16

"Talon guide me," Wren said as he propped himself up with his arms. Through the vents in the roof, he saw the stars amidst the gray smoke that reached up to Sky. About him, a cacophony of snores drowned out all other noise. Famished and parched, the simple act of lifting his torso off the bench was laborious. Wren needed sustenance. Slowly rising and stepping away from the bench, Wren moved slowly to the nearest fire pit where a pot remained in the embers of the dying fire. Grabbing a ladle, Wren stirred about the pot's contents, which were a thick broth stocked with beans, venison and corn. Helping himself to a bowl of the soup, Wren quickly consumed the lukewarm meal along with the remains of corn bread he found on a wooden plate nearby. Slowly, strength returned to his limbs and clarity to his mind. The nightmare still nagging him, Wren finished his meal and then left the longhouse after grabbing a bearskin cloak before he exited.

"By the Oki," Wren whispered as he emerged from the longhouse and step into the village proper. The snow was nearly gone and the temperature seemed more fitting for a warm, autumn day rather a winter's night. "What has happened?"

"Quite a bit, actually," a familiar voice replied. Startled, Wren turned about to find Whisper; she emerged from the shadows on the far side of the Bear Clan's longhouse similarly cloaked in bearskin. Moon's light captured Whisper in her eternal beauty while her voice reverberated her strength. "The summer winds emerged with a vengeance last night, though the chill of winter has been steadily returning since just before nightfall."

"How long have I been asleep?" Wren asked, awed at the pools of melt water that covered area that inches of snow dominated before he slept.

"You've dreamt the last two days away, Featherling," she continued, her revelation as frightening as her use of the name the dream matron scolded Wren for using.

"I am Calling Wren, I am Erie," Wren replied, his conviction clear. He felt pride in his acceptance of his true self. Whisper smiled at his reply and walked up to within a few steps of her love.

"And what does Calling Wren wish?" she asked him, her hopes for their life together renewed.

"I wish to leave with you, to rejoin our people." The lovers then embraced for love and for fear. They both recognized that the guards at the village gates would prevent their escape and openly proclaiming their Erie heritage would mean death.

"What do we do, Wren? How do we escape?"

"I don't know yet, but we will find a way out," Wren replied, his conviction strengthened by the pulsating of Whisper's heart, her chest to his; neither wanted to cease their embrace.

Moon's radiance diminished as clouds passed over, which protected the two Erie from errant eyes. They did not waste the time.

"Two days I've missed. What has happened? Is the Black Robe safe?" Wren looked into Whisper's eyes for hope, but he found none.

"Four of the English and an escort of Onondaga arrived this morning. They've been interrogating your friend all day, and I think they mean to execute him at sunrise." Wren looked off towards the distant lodge where William slept; light emanated through the gaps in the structure's siding.

"Go and pack, whatever foodstuffs you can quietly gather," Wren said as he returned his gaze to Whisper. "Bring a bear cloak for the Black Robe, for the growing cloud cover speaks of a heavy snow from the northern lake."

"You're going to rescue the Black Robe? Why?" Whisper was exasperated, angry. "Why risk us for him?"

"Because he surrendered his life for you and me. I will not abandon him to the English or the Haudenosaunee." She knew the look in his eyes, the stubbornness. There was no turning back. "Gather the supplies, matron of the Turtle Clan and meet me at the front gate, I beg you."

"And what of the guards?"

"Leave them to me."

***

The northern winds escalated with each passing moment. Fortunately, the foreboding force covered Wren's footfalls allowing him to draw close to the lodge undetected. His ear close to the structure's siding, Wren listened for conversations. Beyond the sheets of bark siding, all he could discern, however, was a mixture of unfamiliar dialects spoken with white-kin accents, though Wren heard no hint of the Irishman's voice.

***

William never expected Wren to return. The Jesuit figured that the Bear Clan would not risk Wren aiding him. When evening came after he last saw Wren, a Seneca brought William food. The same Seneca, a young male, returned the next morning and evening with food as well. *Had Wren been executed?* William did not ask about Wren's whereabouts, fearful any inquiry would jeopardize Wren or Wind's Whisper. That second night was the hardest William ever endured. Bound to the lodge's main support pole, William could do nothing but watch as more of the injured were vacated from the lodge while he considered what might have befallen Wren. Then, just as the first rays of the dawn reached the lodge, William fell asleep. Consciousness did not bring hope.

"Do you plan to sleep the whole day away, Jesuit?" a voice asked. William struggled to open his eyes. Given the ever-familiar English accent laced through the words he heard, William was absolutely certain he did not want to wake up.

"Come on, you must eat something," the voice said again. William realized then that his hands were free and he was covered with a blanket. Opening his eyes, he saw a man dressed in a red coat covered by an iron breastplate. The English soldier was warming his hands by the fire.

"Are you all right, Jesuit?" the soldier asked, looking directly at William. The priest remained quiet, uncertain how to play the game he figured had already started. "Strange, a Jesuit who does not understand English. Perhaps Español? You certainly don't look French."

"Español, Si," William answered in the hopes of hiding his accent and true heritage. The soldier continued in Spanish.

"You are a long way from home, priest. Are you lost?"

"No more than you are, colonel," William replied in Spanish as he stood and walked slowly towards the Englishmen.

"You honor me, sir," the colonel said before grasping the priest's hand. "It is well that you know of the New Army and its divisions. Please, join me by the fire." The colonel escorted William to the fire pit where three large stumps were situated, two as chairs and one upon which rested a pot and two wooden cups filled with tea. Sitting on opposite sides of the makeshift table, the colonel gave a cup to William before raising the other cup. "To your health, my dear priest," the colonel said in toast. William raised his glass to the toast before sipping from the cup.

"Tell me something, priest? How do you tolerate these savages?"

"They're a great people, colonel..." William stared at his host, awaiting input from the soldier.

"Colonel Benjamin James, and you?" William had just taken a sip of tea when the question came. He froze in wonder. How would he answer? He thought of fellow priests he previously served with before answering.

"Miguel Mateo, my lord colonel. I am Father Miguel Mateo."

"To your health, Father Mateo," Colonel James said as he raised his cup once more. After downing the remainder of the cup's contents, Colonel James set the cup back on table and then raised his hands towards the fire. "God awful country this is. You Jesuits are certainly rugged men. Well, at least you're alive."

"Milord?" William asked, uncertain where the conversation was headed.

"Many of your order have met quite unfortunate ends, have they not? From what I've been told, you almost met a similar fate as several martyrs amongst the Huron."

"We do as the Holy Father requires." William then drank further from his cup intent on remaining as silent as possible.

"Indeed, Father Mateo. In any event, I'm glad I could assist you in evading such a grotesque end. I wonder, if in return, you would assist me?"

"I'm not sure I could be of any help with military concerns. To be honest, I don't see what use a colonel is in this forsaken land."

"Lord Cromwell sent me here to clarify the French presence throughout this continent. While a military engagement may seem farfetched or useless, Lord Cromwell asked me personally to assess the situation." The evocation of Cromwell's name sent a shiver down William's spine.

"I would imagine you are of great importance for such an assignment, as well as a strategist of high marks," William replied wondering what questions the colonel was about to ask.

"I was a lead architect of several of Lord Cromwell's engagements in Ireland. Savage country, not unlike here, which is what made me a choice candidate for the New World. To that end, I wish to know of the French Fortifications you've visited since arriving from Europe." William's silence was telling. 'Fear not, Father.

I am not here to execute Catholics. I merely wish to know about the resources France has at her disposal."

"I am merely a priest, colonel. The French military personnel shared little with me, especially since I hold no office within the Church. I am literally treated as a nuisance. Frankly, I have little doubt the French know I'm here. They prefer us martyred rather than helping the Indians endure the plagues we brought."

"Unfortunately, Father Mateo, I don't believe you," Colonel James replied as he stood and stepped next to William. "In fact, my dear priest," Colonel James continued, in English," I have no doubt you speak English and God knows how many other languages. Yet, I will get my answers soon enough. Guards!" Three red-coated guards entered the lodge in response to the colonel's summons. "Bind the good priest to the pole."

Chapter 17

Colonel James inflicted repeated lashes to William's back with a whittled branch after the priest was first bound naked to one of the lodge's support posts. William's skin broke open after the third hit, and the priest collapsed to his knees after the seventh hit. Yet, Father William Sullivan's pain sounded after the first hit and resonated throughout the village.

"Do you think the French would waste a moment before turning you or any of your countrymen over to spare the pain, my dear Father Mateo?" Colonel James asked in Spanish after twenty lashes. Speckles of William's blood splattered across the colonel's breastplate, which the English officer seemed to relish. The colonel crouched down next to the priest before asking additional questions. "All I need is an idea of the French fortifications and troop deployments. A few details and your pain will end, Mateo."

"I never made it… to… Quebec City," William said in Spanish. The priest struggled to breathe, but he managed through nonetheless. "I was… captured… by the Iroquois, sent here." The colonel stood and walked to the fire where he warmed his hands once more.

"You make a compelling case, but I still think you are withholding something," Colonel James said, his tone jovial. "I tell you what, rest while I have some tea, and then we'll start again."

The pattern continued throughout the day. William would insist he knew little of the French plans, fortifications or troop strengths. Then, after unleashing a host of wry remarks, Colonel James would whip at the priest's back, though he never again inflicted more than three to five lashes. Ever the English gentleman, the colonel supplied the priest with water and cornbread, but soon William lost all desire for physical refreshment. After his fifth round of lashes, William's mind drifted beyond the present. The crackle of the fire and the scent of charcoal, a source of serenity for William throughout his life, brought the priest to memories of his mother's cooking and nights by the fire when his father told stories of Celtic heroes long since departed from the world. William also remembered the nights in the New World when he slept under the stars, the scent and sound of the campfire harmonizing with the distant call of crickets.

The memories washed away the injuries he accumulated at the colonel's hands.

"I'm ready to come home, Father," William said as the shades of night crept into the lodge. Seconds later, he passed into unconsciousness just as Wren's eye caught sight of the priest through a gap in the lodge's birch bark siding.

***

"Who is in there?" Wren asked. The Erie could neither understand the languages spoken nor place the accents. Concealed against the lodge's sidewall, which faced the palisade, Wren maneuvered in silence while looking for gaps in the bark sheets that covered the structure. Finally he spied the figures who spoke. One, sheathed in a metal plate over a red coat, stood over the other; the other was naked, his back to Wren. The naked man's accent seemed oddly familiar. Memory soon served as Wren recalled the Frenchmen he encountered seasons passed amongst the Wendat. *When did a Frenchman arrive?* The suddenly upraised arm of the Redcoat pulled Wren's attentions away from the naked man. Wren watched a series of arm swings fall upon the naked man, actions followed by audible cries.

"Hail Mary, full of grace!" the naked man cried, not that Wren understood a word. The Redcoat showed no mercy; the arm continued to fall. Wren moved to another section of the wall when he heard additional voices. Finding a bigger gap in the siding, Wren discerned varied headdresses donned by multiple Iroquoians. Feather arrangements amongst the newly arrived marked the new arrivals as a contingent of Seneca and Onondaga. Wren turned his roaming eye back to the Redcoat and his prey. It was then he saw the naked man collapse. It was William.

Wren wanted to yell, to run to his friend's aid, but he knew better. Outnumbered, the Erie awaited the move of his enemies.

***

"Pathetic," Colonel James said as he watched William collapse to the ground, blood seeping from the assorted gashes spread over the priest's back. "Frenchmen have the constitution of women." The colonel then turned his attention to the Iroquoians who entered the lodge. "What is it?" the colonel asked, his annoyance peeked.

"We've been invited to celebrate the morning's festivities with the Snipe Clan," one of the Onondaga's translators replied, stepping forward to address the Redcoat.

"Savages," Colonel James said under his breath, horrified that executions were something to rejoice. "You should have cooperated, priest," Colonel James said turning his attentions back to William. "Now your fate is beyond my control."

Convinced the priest lacked strategic knowledge, Colonel James donned a bearskin cloak offered by a Seneca and then followed the gathered throng into the night.

Once outside, Colonel James stared up to the sky as he adjusted the heavy cloak he now bore. Wet snow started to fall from the gathering clouds emerging from the north.

"Damn this weather," the colonel said as he continued his walk with the provided escort. Hidden in the shadows, Wren stood still as his enemies departed into the growing night. The Erie meanwhile took note of the coming storm, fueled by the moisture of the lake. Wren took comfort in the storm and the cover it would provide during their escape. He just needed to free the Black Robe. After his enemies' footfalls fell silent, Wren moved to the lodge's entrance and through the hide-covered portal, convinced he and his compatriots were moments from freedom. Calling Wren's joy vanished as he found an Onondaga guarding William.

Chapter 18

Wishing to avoid disturbing any of the Bear Clan, Whisper gathered what supplies she could from the end storage area of the Bear Clan's longhouse. After emptying a torso-sized corn-husk basket of its contents, kindling, Whisper refilled the container with several ears of corn and four handfuls of venison jerky stored in covered baskets. For an additional cloak, all she could find was the tatters of a bearskin likely worn by a child. Not daring to risk discovery, Whisper grabbed the bearskin before heading out into the night. Now quite familiar with the village, Wind's Whisper, Erie matron of the Turtle Clan, maneuvered through the village towards the main gate. Once there, she crouched behind a stack of firewood and awaited her love.

***

The coming storm comforted Rising Sun. It was as if Sky was a kindred spirit, angered with the rest of the village.

Standing an unasked vigil, Rising Sun smoke from a English pipe while considering a change.

"At least the English have honor," he said as he thought of traveling with Colonel James back to Cayuga or even Onondaga territory. He envisioned serving the colonel or even the confederacy in its negotiations with the white-kin thereby granting himself the chieftainship he desired. Inhaling another bit of tobacco, Rising Sun placed the small, white clay pipe on the ground before reaching to the firearm his clan received from the colonel. Loaded with powder and a musket ball, the weapon was ready for use. In the morning, the colonel and his entourage said they would instruct the clan on firing and reloading the firearm. Until then, Rising Sun sought familiarity with the weapon's weight rationalizing that he was the clear and only choice for wielding the weapon. Roughly the size of his legs, the firearm seemed unwieldy yet stunted compared to the longer muskets carried by the English themselves. Pushing past that observation, Rising Sun lifted the firearm and aimed at a distant tree, just as one of the colonel's men taught him.

Clad in a cloak made of coyote pelts, Rising Sun found it difficult to aim. Yet, as he shifted his focus between targets, the Seneca found it easier to guide the bulky weapon. From tree tops to stacks of wood, Rising Sun continually refocused until he assured himself the potential "invader" would have fallen. His arm soon tired, Rising Sun rested the butt of the firearm on the ground as he bent low to take up his pipe. Standing, the Seneca again inhaled the tobacco-laced air, a feeling of satisfaction enveloping his spirit with each additional draw of the pipe. Contentment then vanished.

A distant shadow darted into Rising Sun's view. With only a few rays of Moon's light free of the growing cloud cover, Rising Sun struggled to identify the interloper until a stray cast of Moon's light hit the mark.

"Lopi," Rising Sun whispered, now seething with memories of his embarrassment at her hands. Lifting the firearm, Rising Sun melded into the darkness, intent on inflicting his vengeance.

***

The Onondaga guarding William stood taller than any man Wren had known. Having shed his outer garments, the Onondaga's husky physic made clear the daunting task Wren must complete.

"It's never simple," Wren said as he quickly weaved an alternate plan. "I am Featherling, of the Bear Clan," Wren said as he bowed slightly towards the Onondaga now readied for confrontation.

"What do you want, Seneca?" the Onondaga asked, as he raised an iron-tipped spear towards the newcomer.

"I am tasked by the clan matrons to see to your needs. Can I get you some soup and bread?" With a quick glance to the ground, Wren could see William starting to move.

"A meal would be appreciated, Featherling."

"Here, let me build up your fire before I leave," Wren said as he maneuvered passed the Onondaga. The Onondaga's spear now lowered, Wren felt at ease as he grabbed three logs from the lodge's stockpile of wood and placed the leg-sized logs on the fire. A flurry of embers lofted into the air with the new weight the fire bared. The priest nearby, Wren glanced towards his friend; William's eyes were open. Wren winked at the priest.

"The fire is fine," the Onondaga said, his annoyance building.

"Very well," Wren replied as he exited the lodge and walked right to the stack of firewood nearest the lodge. Grabbing four large logs, Wren turned and walked back into the structure.

"Just let me replenish the pile before I get you something to eat," Wren said as he walked by the Onondaga, dropping one of the logs as he passed by. As Wren hoped, the Onondaga picked up the dropped firewood and brought it to the pile.

"Thank you for the help," Wren said as the Onondaga set the log on top of the wood stack, his right hand grasped tightly around a stout log. "Eriehronon," Wren said after the Onondaga nodded and turned to resume his vigil. The Onondaga turned for combat at the call of the Erie name, but Wren moved faster. One swing of the log to the Onondaga's head rendered the enemy unconscious. Dropping the log, Wren ran to William's side.

"William, are you okay? What can I do?" Wren, exasperated, gently cradled his friend in his arms all the while fearing the priest's life was slipping away. William simply groaned as Wren turned him over, the priest's eyes tightly shut. Yet, as Wren despaired of flight now, William's eyes opened and reflected a strength, an endurance that was far from extinguished.

"You know, that cornbread was really good," William said, his accent back to that which he used the last time they spoke. "You wouldn't happen to have more, would you?"

The two men laughed, an action that suddenly caused William to cough and groan once more.

"Can you move, my friend?" Wren asked knowing that each moment they rested stole precious time from their escape.

"I'll... I'll be all right. I've been whipped worse than this by English hands. The colonel's slashes and commentary were so weak... I... I fell asleep from boredom." William followed his jest with his customary smile. Wren smiked as he helped the priest to his feet.

"You Irish are a strange people, you know that?"

"Never said we weren't," William replied as Wren helped the priest back into his clothes, boots and hooded cloak. Then, grabbing a stout pole from the woodpile for a walking stick for William, the two made their way to the lodge portal. Once outside, Wren stopped their flight and looked back towards the dwelling they spent much of their recent days in.

"Stay here just a moment," Wren said as he helped William secure his stance. Wren then quickly disappeared back into the lodge while William braced against the growing wind and falling snow, his impromptu staff greatly aiding his resistance. In little time, Wren emerged from the lodge dragging the unconscious Onondaga out with him.

"Let's move, Black Robe," Wren said as he wrapped his right arm about William's back for added support.

"We can't leave him to die in the elements!" William exclaimed. We are better than that. Drag him back inside." Seconds later flames shot through gaps in the lodge's siding and quickly lapped up parts of the walls. "Never mind," William said as he moved along with Wren away from the fire.

Wren and William moved amongst the shadows as voices of alarm carried into the night. Glancing back towards the rising inferno, Wren saw several figures reach the unconscious Onondaga and drag him beyond the potential reach of the fire. Turning there attentions towards the gate, Wren and William watched as the two guards fled from their posts towards the fire; escape now seemed certain.

"Why did you change your voice?" Wren asked as they drew within feet of the gate. William chuckled a bit before responding.

"Not the best French accent, but it served its purpose. As the Onondaga hate your people, so do the English hate mine. The difference is, if the Onondaga discover you are Erie, their anger will be directed solely at you. If the English find out I'm Irish, they won't hesitate to annihilate

this entire village for allowing me to live."
Again William had saved Wren and Whisper.

"What are you?" Wren asked William, the
Erie smiling in disbelief. Here was not the Black
Robe Iroquoians spoke of with fear, dread. Here
was a man, a friend, a comrade, and nothing
more.

"I am William," the priest replied as the two
friends embraced amidst a collective laughter.

"Quiet!" Wind's Whisper scolded in little
more then a whisper. Her reprimand ceased the
men's revelry and returned the seriousness of the
moment. "I gathered what I could," Whisper
said as she handed the tattered fur to Wren. He
went to remove his cloak when William grabbed
the tattered outer garment.

"This will suffice. Let's go," William said
as he draped the fur across his back and moved
on towards the gate, Wren and Whisper following behind. Once beyond the gate, Wren took
the lead as they neared the tree line. Within the
radiance of Moon's light, Wren watched wind-
cast snow coalesce into a familiar shape. Again,
the great fish appeared before Calling Wren, but
for a mere second.

"Beware," Talon called out, the spirit's
voice resonating through Wren's mind. Chilled
by the warning, Wren spun around in time to see

Rising Sun emerging from the gate, the Seneca's firearm aimed at Whisper.

"Whisper!" Wren exclaimed as he bolted towards his love. He ran two steps before the firearm went off.

Chapter 19

The musket ball pierced through the air with ease, its trajectory to Wind's Whisper unimpeded by bushes or trees. Yet, William struck first.

The Jesuit heard a new set of footfalls behind them as they neared the trees. Glancing back, he saw Rising Sun lift the musket. Without delay, the priest ran to Whisper and positioned behind her a heartbeat after the musket fired, the projectile striking William's back, which forced him to the ground. Whisper turned and crouched to render what aid she could to the priest without concern for additional volleys. Wren had other plans. Glancing at his fallen friend, Wren ran towards Rising Sun. Having dropped the firearm, Rising Sun unsheathed an iron dagger he received from the English. The two Iroquoians slammed into each other and onto the ground where they rolled about in the snow, each now grasping at the dagger, trying to guide the blade's path. Rising Sun was stronger, which meant Wren had little time before he was overpowered.

"*So close to freedom*," Wren thought as he continued to wrestle for any advantage over the Seneca.

"Erie filth!" Rising Sun exclaimed as he too moved about in hopes of inflicting a painful death on Wren and Whisper. "Lopi will be mine again!" Wren's fears for Wind's Whisper elevated instantly, renewing his vigor. Yet, he still struggled against the weight and muscle of his adversary. Wren's hope of victory was slipping. In the distance, he also heard collective shouts, which suggested villagers were running to investigate the gunfire. They were out of time.

"*They betrayed the Oki*," a voice said, carried on the growing wind. It sounded more like a chorus than a solitary individual speaking. As silence drowned out everything, visions of the great fish, the hawk and Wren's father flashed about his mind. Then, as Rising Sun turned Wren over on his back, Wren stared upward, past the falling snowflakes and into the maw of Sky.

"*They betrayed the Oki*," the voices, now clearly a chorus, cried out. With his hands gripped tightly round the dagger's handle, Wren looked into Rising Sun's eyes. Glancing inches lower, Wren then saw Talon dangling from the Seneca's neck and, beyond that, Wren's peripheral vision spied a chert dagger with an antler handle attached to Rising Sun's belt. Releasing his grip on the iron dagger, Wren twisted out of the blade's path, which was propelled into the ground by the Seneca's weight. Rising Sun recovered quickly, pushing himself up to his knees. With sole possession of the iron dagger, he looked to end their battle, but Wren had other plans. Yanking the chert knife from Rising Sun's belt, Wren plunged the stone blade into Rising Sun's chest and heart.

"For the Oki, and my wife," Wren said as Rising Sun released the iron dagger and toppled to the snow-covered ground. For a brief moment, the adversaries stared into each other's eyes. Then, as Rising Sun drew his last breath, his eyes closed, his life expended. Wren look to Sky, giving thanks through his silence. The Erie defender then reach to Rising Sun's neck and jerked free Talon. Standing, he looked at the amulet and took comfort in its familiar feel. Renewed shouts from the village prevented further meditation and increased the urgency of their actions. He ran to Whisper who hovered over the Black Robe.

"Is he alive?" Wren asked, fearing the worst.

"I've gotten worse injuries from fights with my brother," William said. The two men chuckled. The Irishman never ceased to joke.

"Let's go!" Whisper exclaimed as she pulled William to his feet with Wren's help. They then

fled together into the nearest outcropping of conifers, both Erie supporting William, just as an
enclave of Senecas, Onondagas and the colonel
emerged from the gate.

"The projectile embed itself in the Black
Robe's shoulder," Whisper said once they were
hidden. It'll be difficult for him to move."

"Leave me here, Wren," William said as he
pushed out of their grasp. "Go home." William
leaned against a silver maple as he tried to catch
his breath. Whisper had wrapped the tattered
bearskin cloak about William's shoulder, which
provided a temporary bandage.

"I will not leave you to die," Wren protest-
ed. William held up his left arm, his palm pressing against Wren's chest to prevent the Erie from
moving closer.

"I am a Celt, Wren. My people have long
lived amongst the trees. Never will I be caught
by adversaries in the wild, particularly not by a
group led by English," William said as a smirk
crossed his face. "Flee to your village. I will
lead the Senecas to the north, but you must warn
your people." Wren remained still even as their
enemies' voices grew louder, closer. "Your matron needs you, Wren," William said, his tone
firm and serious. "As do your people." Wren
knew his friend was right.

"Take care and travel safe, William," Wren said as he stepped back from the Black Robe.

"You do the same, Calling Wren of the Erie."

"We must go," Whisper said as she pulled on Wren's arm. Turning around, Wren moved onward, his hand tightly grasped to Whisper's.

"Wren!" William called out; the two Erie stopped and turned back in response. "Tell your people to flee until they are truly ready to stand. Though it take a thousand turns of the seasons, do not stand until you are ready. Now go... live free, live Erie."

For the last time, Wren looked to his friend and bowed. Wind's Whisper and Calling Wren then proceeded on into the wilderness, the Jesuit left alone in their wake.

"May God watch over you both," Father William Sullivan prayed as the shouts of the enemy drew closer. "Now to contend with this rabble," the Celt whispered as he melded into the trees.

***

Fire blanketed the entire lodge by the time Colonel James reached the far end of the village. The roaring fire, its ferocity augmented by the wailing winds that fueled its fury, continually launched embers, which the Seneca frantically tried to stamp out. In a village whose wooden buildings stood so tightly packed, such a fire could destroy everything. Yet, Colonel James failed to see the alarm as his focus remained on the prisoner.

"Where is the priest?" the colonel asked a lieutenant who reached the vicinity of the lodge first.

"They believe an Erie captive freed him."

"Then let's move before the snow covers their tracks."

"Milord, the snow is picking up. Should we not wait until…"

Colonel James glared at his subordinate, with ice-blue eyes that abruptly ended the query.

"Patrol, make ready!" The lieutenant exclaimed as he made for the longhouse where their supplies were stored. In minutes, Colonel James, his officers and a troop of Iroquoians were out the front gate, torches in hand. Stopping at the remains of Rising Sun, Colonel James looked about for footprints that could guide their pursuit.

"Here, milord!" another lieutenant shouted. "A solitary set of prints." The lieutenant then crouched down to further examine the track. "Given the heel print, I'd say this is the mark of the Jesuit, milord," the young man said as Colonel James reached him. The colonel then looked in the distance, hoping to see a glimpse of his quarry; no sign appeared.

"Take these men and hunt him down, lieutenant," Colonel James commanded. Bowing his reply, the lieutenant spoke to one of the assembled Onondaga, their translator, who relayed the command to the others. The pursuers were off in an instant.

Now alone, Colonel James watched as his men followed the Iroquoians into the night. He caught glimpses of the search party whenever moonlight broke through the clouds and snow.

"Such a waste of my gifts," he said as he contemplated his reliance on the savages he deemed beneath him. Footfalls from behind him ended his self-pity. Turning, he gazed into the face of Father Sullivan.

"My dear, priest," Colonel James said in French. "Masterfully done." The colonel chuckled as he considered the priest's trickery. "You are to be commended. Now, if you would be so kind as to tell me where your Erie coconspirators went."

"A good question, that," William replied in English. It took half a heartbeat for Colonel James to denote William's accent.

"You Irish bastard!" the officer screamed while unsheathing the saber strapped to his belt.

William was faster. Working through his intensive injuries, William brought up his staff and slammed the oak limb's butt into the colonel's forehead. Colonel James fell backwards into the growing layers of snow, unconscious before he hit the ground. William then painfully crouched over and listened; the colonel's breathing remained strong.

"May God forgive you and me for our angry actions," Father William prayed as he made the sign of the Cross. After propping the English officer up against a nearby elder maple, William covered his now snoring enemy with the tattered cloak he donned. In the distance, voices of the other English officers could be heard; they were barking orders at the Seneca and Onondaga. William stood and looked at the Iroquoians as they led the English onward.

"Poor fools," William said as he picked up his staff while reflecting on the Seneca's alliance with England. "Made a pact with the devil you did. You'd been better off siding with the French." Looking one last time at the officer, William moved off south, softly singing every step of the way.

Will you remember me in time,
Debra Arun…

Will you pray for me o'er the years,
Debra Arun…

My heart, my heart, cries for thee,
Debra Arun…

For we must part whilst in this world,
Debra Arun…

Chapter 20

Wren and Whisper's journey west grew easier with each passing day. While the cloud cover indicated snow was bombarding Seneca lands, the western lands sat under clear skies, a welcome circumstance for the two Erie. At night, they huddled close under conifers and ate sparingly of the food Wind's Whisper collected. Then, three days after their flight from captivity, Wren eyed familiar landmarks; home was near.

In one more turn of Sun, the lovers saw the palisade of their village. Little snow covered the surrounding ground and the temperatures allowed them to remove their cloaks.

"We've done it," Wren said as he saw smoke billow forth from vents in the nearest longhouses. The sight made it appear as if their village was at peace and free of the violence that raked across the northeast.

"No, my dear husband," Wind's Whisper said as she turned to her love. "You did this. You made this possible."

Grasping hands, Wren and Whisper trudged along the remaining distance, relieved to be home at last.

***

The day of Wren and Whisper's return was warmer than any day the village elders could recall. Men, women and children danced and sang, jubilant that two of theirs returned against great odds.

"You certainly took your time, my Calling Wren," Rock's Blood said as he embraced his son. Wren just held his father tight, speaking not a word and wanting the moment to last forever. Matron Sulvas quickly arranged a great feast for the village and a traditional wedding ceremony for the returned, but Wren and Whisper knew the celebration would be short-lived. The next day, Whisper called the matrons together, along with Rock's Blood, to listen to Wren's tale and of the growing danger the Haudenosaunee represented.

"They have weapons, resources and numbers we cannot match, matrons, and the Black Robe said that more English come with every tide," Wren said to the assembly. "We must leave our lands behind if we are to survive." His brow soaked in sweat, he awaited, like his father, for the matrons to permit further discussion.

"And you feel you can trust this *Irish*?" one of the gathered matrons asked, her tone harsh.

"I was there, and I trust him," Wind's Whisper replied, standing to face the matrons alongside her husband. "And I can vouch that this Black Robe sought to aid our people." Wind's Whisper's frosty gaze cooled the fire of the dissenting matrons while Wind's words brought understanding. "If we stay, we will lose everything. The only hope the Erie have is to return well into the southwest, to regions many Iroquoians once called home. There we can gather strength."

"And leave our hunting grounds and our fields to the Haudenosaunee?" asked another matron who blanched at the thought of finding new lands to inhabit.

"The Seneca will likely take control of the land, and they will keep it whole, which is what the Oki would ultimately want," Matron Sulvas said, standing up from her seat amongst the matrons. She then scanned the faces of the gathered before looking to her husband. "What does our war chief think of our choices?" she asked.

"We cannot win," he replied, sullenly. Diseases of the white-kin grow more virulent as the seasons progress, and the Haudenosaunee gather strength and firearms while our numbers dwindle, as do our resources. It is my belief that we will be overrun by next autumn. The Oki have graced us with good weather," Rock's Blood added as he looked about the Deer Clan's longhouse, now void of all save those gathered for the assembly. The few lit fire pits set an ominous aura for the proceedings, which Wren thought helped their case. "The bulk of our village should flee southwest while the weather holds. I will remain and coordinate the evacuation of the other Erie village as well as the defenders who remain with me. That should give all of you the chance to establish relations with nations who will have us."

"You would leave us defenseless?" the Turtle Clan matron asked, fearful at the loss of their war chief and any of the defenders.

"We will have Calling Wren to guide us," Wind's Whisper said with pride as she looked into his eyes. "My husband will lead us on." Her words brought pride to Wren's parents and received nods of agreement from the other matrons. The plan was accepted.

**

"Talon," Rock's Blood said as he held his son's amulet, his finger tracing along the tooth's serrated edge. "I'm glad you discovered its identity before your departure. Now I know what name to listen for in the wind," he added as he handed the amulet back to Calling Wren. "He and Rook are bonded as are you and I, Wren. It is a bond that Sky will never permit to break."

Standing at the village's gate the next morning, Wren and Rock's Blood watched as one hundred thirty-seven of the village's residents marched southward with few personal items and a minimal amount of dried meat and vegetables. Rock's Blood looked on as his son slipped on the hide strap that bore Talon. With a new raccoon cloak and maple staff, Wren reminded the village's war chief of his younger days. He wished to travel with Wren, but his duties prevented it.

"You should be beyond the range of our lake's snow within two days if you keep true south," Rock's Blood said as the end of the line of departing villagers neared. Father and son looked to one another, fear and pride reflected in both their eyes. "Look forward, not backward, Calling Wren. Lead the people forward."

"What of you, the others…"

"Your duties are with them," Rock's Blood said nodding to the line of Erie heading south. "I've sent runners to the Susquehannock; we'll find sanctuary there for some of our people."

"And the rest of our people?"

"We will stand, Wren, and hold back our enemies as long as possible. For now, you need to see to the safety of your charges. Whisper and the other matrons with you will guide you well; trust in their judgment." Wren turned and looked out over those marching southwards. He caught a glimpse of Whisper, her smile ever-present since her return to Erie soil. There was hope in her smile. Turning again to his father, Wren saw how much his father had aged in the previous weeks, saddened by the losses from the Seneca attack and Wren's supposed death. Yet, in the last two days, Rock's Blood seemed re-newed, like a young defender set to prove his worth to the Oki and the matrons.

"Goodbye, my dear boy," Rock's Blood said as he embraced Wren one last time. "You are my pride, Calling Wren." Wren hugged his fa-ther tightly, before stepping back. Though tears flowed from Wren's eyes, he smiled at his father, but Wren could not speak. He nodded once more to Rock's Blood before turning and follow-ing the path behind the others. Then, as he neared the first bend in the path, Wren stopped and turned back. Sun bathed the village with its full light, but even that intense light paled in Rock's Blood presence. Wren's voice returned.

"Live free, live Erie, father," Wren called out before proceeding forward on the path.

***

Calling Wren never saw his father again. Whispers of Rock's Blood's exploits filtered southward as the people fled. Some said Rock's Blood joined with remnants of the Wendat to attack the Haudenosaunee from the north. Others brought word of Rock's Blood joining with the disease and war decimated nations of the south to strike at the heart of Iroquoia, existing as a tribe known as the Black Minqua. Calling Wren sought not to extract truth from the tales. He simply spoke of his father's bravery and the sacrifice of the warriors that remained to provide the Erie with a chance to escape and survive, as the Erie have.

For centuries the Erie lived, ever remaining a step ahead of all enemies, dwelling for years or decades until a need to move on arose. The matrons still direct the people, though, with each generation, a new guide provides the vision for action. Whether woman or man, the guide is named 'Calling Wren.'

Epilogue

"Challenge accepted," Jack said as he worked on the damaged neck of his Baroque guitar. After first replacing the instrument's gut strings, he noticed a hairline crack on the neck near the guitar's body. "Well, can't play without a guitar," Jack added as he settled down by his campfire for what figured to be a daylong endeavor.

Like a surgeon, Jack removed the strings and defective neck after which he worked on a replacement. Without a spare readily available, Jack chopped down an appropriate-sized limb from a nearby oak before sitting on a large rock positioned within range of his campfire's warmth. There, deep within the woodlands south of Iroquois territory, Jack worked in secret, his goal to reach areas further south before the Onondaga, Oneida or Mohawk noticed him and prevented Jack from ultimately reaching Jamestown. After months of travel across the Atlantic, in quarters leaving no breathing room for even the rodents, Jack soon treasured the openness of the New World's forests. Certainly not

Ireland, yet the North American forests were lovely, inspiring, and the perfect setting for Jack to write music and perform in.

Jack, a son of the Carey Clan, looked to the New World and the fables he envisioned just waiting to be learned and told to townsfolk and gentry throughout Europe. His voice and music paid his fare over the seas, and now he planned to walk about the New World in search of tales of noble quests, heroic tragedies and comedies that often befell noblemen who clumsily staggered about the woodlands.

"What harm could befall us," Jack remembered a number of passengers saying boldly as they neared the shores of the Plymouth Colony, as if the Pilgrims' trials were already beyond memory. In fact, it was the calamitous occurrences surrounding the Plymouth and Roanoke settlements that inspired Jack's quest.

"Now, if I could just fix this damn guitar," he cursed as the first neck he fashioned proved too cracked to suffice. The second leg-sized branch he secured proved better suited for a guitar neck. Jack's reconstruction efforts well underway by noon, he took time to fish, eat and rest. His camp, located on a knoll just above a creek teeming with rock bass, was an idyllic setting for the minstrel to compose poems and songs corresponding to all he learned thus far on his travels. With a lean-to for shelter and ample wood for his fire, it proved the perfect camp. He dreaded the fact that he needed to leave the following morning to keep pace with his plans.

"What a land," Jack said as he took up his wounded guitar and again contemplated the richness of the environment. Thoughts of further adventures soon pushed the minstrel to continue to repair the guitar. Finally, as the shades of night crept back into the sky, Jack finished his repairs. He put the guitar to work at once.

Strumming the replaced gut chords with a little hesitation at first, Jack broke into verses of his piece about Plymouth and his evasion of the dreaded Iroquois. With the crackling of the fire and the chirps of crickets as accompaniment, minstrel Jack Carey played for the stars, moon and trees, his tune a perfect fit for the wild that lay about him.

"Quite the distance from home, minstrel," a voice called out. Jack ceased playing and stood armed with a flintlock pistol.

"Come out!" Jack ordered as he aimed about, looking for signs of movement. From the shadows emerged a hooded and cloaked figure that initiated memories of old, forgotten histories. "Druid," Jack said as he lowered his pistol.

"Hardly, my dear sir." The cloaked figure said, his eyes hidden by the shadows cast from his hood. "A Jesuit and nothing more am I."

"An Irish Jesuit?" Jack asked as he approached the man.

"To find a countryman here is certainly not what I expected," Father William Sullivan said as he removed his hood, wincing as he did so. In turn, William walked forward, but his footing and consciousness quickly faded. He only remembered the sight of the minstrel running towards him.

***

"Wake up, Father," Jack said as he shook the priest. William, his body shrouded by pain, tried to ignore consciousness. He preferred the fleeting memories of the friendships he had made with Wren and the Wendat. Consciousness would not be ignored, however.

Opening his eyes, the Jesuit observed a man standing over him, a man clad in a white, linen shirt and brown, wool coat. The man, appearing to be roughly William's age, had short, dark brown hair, a goatee, and blue eyes, much like William's brother.

"For Heaven's sake, will you ever wake?" the minstrel asked. William fought through to consciousness, shaking off his tired eyes, blinking until all was clear.

"You wouldn't happen to have some tea, or maybe a drop of whiskey, would you." The man laughed.

"You're definitely not French, Father," the minstrel replied before elevating William's torso so he could drink warm tea from a copper cup. "We'll see about the whiskey when you're more able, Father." William nodded in reply as Jack lowered him back to the ground. Darkness was encroaching on their camp, which startled the priest.

"How long have I…"

"You've slept for two days, Father. I removed the musket ball from your shoulder. You were lucky; it was made from pewter. Had it been lead, I'd be burying you instead of dressing the wound." The man's tone was comforting; the Irish accent helped matters.

"I'm Father William Sullivan," William said as he struggled to raise his right hand.

"My name is Jack Carey," the minstrel said as he gently grabbed the priest's hand in his and lowered the priest's arm to the ground. "You should rest for now. We can get acquainted tomorrow.

"Bless you, Jack," Father William whispered as sleep took hold.

William's strength continued to build over the following two days, reassuring Jack that the priest was ready to move on. Yet, Jack also sensed the priest was struggling with worry. He looked to music to help the priest.

"Have you yourself played an instrument, Father?" Jack asked as he served the priest a stew of rabbit and tubers.

"In my youth, I played the recorder. My parents required us all to play and sing in the Church choir. They felt it was a great way to reach God and better enjoy life." William then proceeded to eat a few spoonfuls of the stew while Jack rustled around in his backpack. Seconds later, the minstrel handed an old recorder to William. Made of stained boxwood, the recorder looked much like those William played back home. Setting down his bowl, William gently accepted the recorder with great care. Scanning the instrument's surface revealed minute stress in the wood; fractures and bruises repaired with wood, shavings and lacquer.

"I don't know what is troubling you Father William, but I sense some secret has you torn inside. You need not explain what it is, but I suggest you play through it. Let the recorder talk for you, and you will find freedom and peace."

Father Sullivan thought over the minstrel's words and smiled. The minstrel talked of freedom as did the Erie. "Live free," was Wren and Redwing's maxim.

"Live free," William said as he brought the recorder to his lips. After minutes of reacquainting himself with the instrument and its key, William pieced together notes in patterns that felt fitting to his experiences with Wren and the Erie. In time, Jack joined in, strumming his guitar in perfect harmony to William's lament. The tune secretly spoke of the Erie, a tale of their glory, and resonated through the woodlands awaiting the day a new Erie tale would unfold.

www.ingramcontent.com/pod-product-compliance
Lightning Source LLC
Chambersburg PA
CBHW052033260626
47163CB00006B/231